CHRISTMAS BY CANDLELIGHT

Two Regency Holiday Novellas

BESTSELLING AUTHOR

ANDREA PICKENS

OLIVERHEBERBOOKS

This title was previously published

0 9 8 7 6 5 4 3 2 1

LOST AND FOUND

CHAPTER 1

"A curse on Christmas."

Nicholas Wrenfax, Viscount Killingworth, was not in the habit of swearing, but he tacked on a rather colorful expletive as he squinted through the pelting sleet and fought to keep his phaeton from running off the road. The night was black as Hades—which seemed particularly appropriate, for at that very moment Hades was just the spot to which he wanted to toss his father, along with Lord Castlereagh and the entire Foreign Office.

Tugging up the sodden collar of his driving coat, he tightened his hold on the ribbons, trying to keep a grip on his growing anger. He had, after all, been well schooled in reining in his feelings. From the time he was in leading strings, his father, a distinguished diplomat, had stressed the importance of being ruled by reason rather than emotion.

Duty over desire.

It was a lesson Nicholas had learned well, having had an

admirable man to emulate. The Earl of Royster was esteemed by all who knew him as a man of high-minded principle and unyielding devotion to duty. Ever since he could remember, Nicholas had wanted to march in his father footsteps. He had applied himself diligently to his studies, and after garnering high honors at Oxford, had chosen to accept a position—granted, a very junior position—with the Home Office while most of his friends had larked off to London to sow their wild oats.

He knew that a number of them considered him a stick-in-the-mud for never kicking up his heels. But the weight of government responsibilities and family expectations kept his feet planted firmly on the ground. He felt he must toe the line...

Even when that line seemed at times to be rigidly straight and pinchingly narrow.

Toe the line—yes, that explained why, curse the holidays, he was racing toward London in a freezing rainstorm, feeling cold, wet and miserable, when instead he should be stretched out by the fire at his best friend's country estate, feeling snug warm and pleasantly foxed on the case of excellent port that had just been brought up from the cellars.

Nicholas shifted on his perch, uncomfortably aware of his father's request tucked in the pocket of his waistcoat—its elegant parchment and copperplate script now reduced to a sodden squish. Or rather, he corrected himself grimly, his father's *order* to rush back to Town. For despite the sugar coating of the words, the note of command had oozed from the pen strokes like the filling of a Christmas sweetmeat.

He still had a sour taste in his mouth from rereading it during the brief stop he had made at an inn several hours ago. Not that the text needed any elaborate analysis. Its message was perfectly clear. The younger Wrenfax was urgently needed for a special assignment of great importance. So Nicholas was expected to present himself without delay to take part in a whirl of holiday parties—where he was to pay court to the ward of an influential foreign count.

The match was perfect on paper, reasoned his father. The young lady's lineage and looks were of the highest order, and a union would ensure a crucial alliance for the British government. And seeing that Nicholas had shown no particular preference for any of the ladies currently on the Marriage Mart, what possible objection could he have for his father's making a prudent and practical match?

What possible objection, indeed! Nicholas's exasperated snort echoed the complaint from his tired team of greys. Just because he had been too occupied with official duties to give any thought to choosing a wife did not mean he wished to relinquish the right to control his own personal life.

Damnation. Perhaps for once in his life. . .

His mood turned even grimmer as the sleet changed to thick, wet flakes. This was courting disaster, he thought darkly as a gusting wind lashed his face. He had better come upon some sign of civilization soon. His horses were starting to stumble and his own limbs were fast turning numb. Nicolas blinked, trying to see through the swirling snow, but ice clung to his lashes, turning the surroundings to naught but an ominous blur. Still, it soon became clear that the road was taking a steeper twist, and drifts were beginning to slow his progress to a mere crawl.

Worst of all, he had a sneaking suspicion that he had taken a wrong turn back at the last fork.

A pox on Edmund for suggesting a shortcut to the London road!

And a pox on his own miserable hide for allowing himself to be spurred into making such an ill-judged journey.

Nicolas let another oath slip from his lips. He didn't normally embark on any endeavor without careful thought and preparations, but the note of urgency in his father's letter had caused him to abandon his usual sense of caution. Urged on by his friends, he had decided to dash down to Town alone, leaving his valet and luggage to follow in the much slower—and safer—travelling coach.

With a shake of the frozen reins, he tried to coax his team to a brisker pace. However, the phaeton was having more and more difficulty in plowing through the drifting snow. As the wheels hit a deep rut, causing a sharp skid, one of the exhausted horses stumbled and pulled up lame.

Jumping down from his perch, Nicholas quickly freed it from the tangled traces. Though tired and shivering himself, he took a moment to calm both animals, and then readjusted the harness for the straitened circumstances. He would go on for another mile or so on foot, he decided, guiding the team over the fast-disappearing road. If he didn't come to some sort of shelter, he would have to improvise. It wouldn't be the first time he had been forced to rough it in the wilds. Most of his acquaintances assumed he did nothing but sit behind a desk and shuffle papers, but his diplomatic mission to Lisbon had actually entailed several forays to meet with partisan fighters. If he ended up being trapped in the storm, Nicolas was confident he had the practical skills to survive.

However, it appeared that Luck had not entirely abandoned him. Rounding a bend, he caught sight of a faint light up ahead. With a muttered prayer of thanks, he stepped up his struggle through the deepening drifts and a short while later managed to limp into the narrow coaching yard of a small inn.

A rap on the stable door roused no response. Though miserably wet and thoroughly exhausted, Nicholas rubbed down his horses, and scrounged up some grain and water for them before trudging to the tavern entrance—where yet again, his knock went unanswered.

His temper, already frayed to a single thread, suddenly snapped.

"Damnation!" Smacking his shoulder to the door, Nicholas grabbed the latch and slammed his way inside. "Is there no one to give a gentleman a hand around here?" he bellowed, stamping the snow from his boots. That his toes now felt frozen into solid blocks of ice did nothing to improve his mood.

A moment later, a balding man bustled out from a side parlor. "Forgive me, sir," he mumbled, wiping his hands on his apron. "We rarely get much traffic from Quality at this time of night, and I was just serving a meal to another unexpected guest."

Nicholas doubted the isolated inn got many visits at any hour of the day. And judging by the rough-planked floor and rustic furnishings, he imagined his short stay was going to be an awfully unpleasant one.

"I will be wanting a room," he snapped. "Preferably one without fleas."

The innkeeper cringed as Nicholas gave him his name.

""I—I shall do my best to see that you are comfortable, milord. Shall you be wanting a meal as well, sir?"

"Just a bottle of brandy," muttered Nicolas. "Assuming it hasn't been watered down with horse piss."

"Yes, milord—er, no, milord." Confused, and clearly intimidated, the man edged back a step before recalling his duties and returning to snap up the small valise by Nicholas's feet. "If you would care to follow me upstairs, milord. . ."

Feeling a bit ashamed of himself, Nicholas fell in step behind the fellow. Though he was tired and frustrated, there was no call to be so arrogantly rude. "I apologize for my outburst," he said on reaching his room. That the spill of candlelight showed it to be quite neat, with freshly ironed linens on the narrow bedstead only made him feel more like a prig.

"What with the hellish weather, the journey has been a nightmare," he went on, "I fear my nerves are rather frayed." The one consolation, he told himself, was that things could not get any worse.

"I quite understand, milord," replied the innkeeper.

"The storm blew in from nowhere, but I daresay it will clear off by morning and you will be able to continue on your way."

Nicholas devoutly hoped so. Christmas was only two days off and from the way his father had phrased the request, his goose would be cooked—along with the rest of the holiday feast—if he didn't show up at Wrenfax House for the gala ball.

"Are you sure there is nothing else I can get for you, sir?"

"Thank you, but no. Just the brandy."

As it was, Nicholas barely managed to stay awake long enough to toss back a glass of the warming spirits before crawling under the bedcovers and falling into an exhausted sleep.

Arrogant man.

The young lady taking her meal in the private parlor couldn't help but overhear the peevish exchange. *And odiously ill tempered to boot.* Why, the stomping of his boots had nearly rattled the door to her dining alcove off its hinges. Had she been the innkeeper, she would have been tempted to respond with a kick of her own—aimed right at the pompous prig's rump!

But then, Anna Wintergrove Fedorova was not feeling in charity with *any* overbearing male at the moment.

Setting aside her tea, Anna looked down at her uncle's letter. How dare he order her back to London, as if she were naught but a mare, to be put up for auction at Tattersall's and sold to the highest bidder?

A foolish question, of course. The answer was staring her right in the face, the bold black script a mocking reminder of how little control she had over her own life.

Oh, if only she had her independence!

She would trade her vast fortune, her august pedigree and celebrated looks in a heartbeat for a bit of unfettered freedom. For months, she had been looking forward to escaping from her regimented life in London—if only for a short interlude—and spending the holidays with a dear school friend.

But duty, in the form of her rigid guardian uncle, had suddenly summoned her back to Town. And no one but no one dared disobey Count Yevgeny Gilpin Fedorov.

Anna made a face. The English acted as though her uncle had a great black bear chained in his study, ready to eat anyone who had the gall to disagree with him. The Count certainly looked like a fearsome predator from the steppes with his great black beard and flashing Cossack eyes. Granted, the beard was neatly trimmed, and the roar was a cultured baritone that could converse on art and music in seven different languages. A confidante of the Tsar, Fedorov had been in London for months, handling a series of delicate and demanding negotiations between Britain and Russia. Not that she had seen much of him. Save for the occasional soiree at their Grosvenor Square townhouse, where she served as his hostess, the count was rarely at home.

What with his travels and his duties, Uncle Yevgeny had

been a rather distant figure of authority since the death of her English mother and Russian father had left him her legal guardian. But then, he had not really been required to devote much attention to her. Her life had been very well ordered—for years she had attended an exclusive boarding school for young ladies outside of London, and lived the rest of the year with her Russian grandmother on a vast estate near St. Petersburg.

But now that she had been out of the schoolroom for several years, her uncle's attitude was becoming decidedly less laissez-faire.

After two whirlwind Seasons at the Russian Imperial Court, where she had driven him to distraction by rejecting marriage proposals from a number of extremely eligible noblemen, he had threatened to put his foot down. If she could not make up her mind, he warned, he would do it for her.

A sigh escaped Anna's lips. Uncle Yevgeny meant well, but he was of the Old Guard, for whom marriage was a matter of strategic alliances. *Money. Power. Land.* His long and distinguished government career, coupled with the interminable war against Napoleon that was still raging through Europe, had only reinforced the importance of tangible assets. He simply did not seem to understand that happiness could not be negotiated in quite the same way as a border dispute. Dispassionate reason was all very well when it came to compromising over slivers of earth.

But when it came to matters of the heart...

She felt a tiny lurch in her chest. She did not wish to settle for a match because it tallied up well on paper. She had been courted according to the rules—impressive bouquets, flowery poetry, effusive compliments on her looks and manners. It was all so. . . expected. As were the gentlemen themselves. They were all so perfectly proper, perfectly polished, perfectly suitable.

And perfectly boring.

Not a one had shown a spark of unique character or spirit.

And so she had begged her uncle for more time and he had grudgingly agreed that she might accompany him to London for the winter months. In March, it would be on to Vienna, by which time he had made it clear that he expected her to make a final decision.

But the arrival of his letter had abruptly revoked the reprieve.

Its message was as cruel a Christmas gift as a lump of cold, hard coal. She must return immediately to London, in order to be courted over the holiday season by a perfectly proper English lord. If she refused, she would have to return in the new year to the household of her imperious grandmother, where the family would take charge of arranging a traditional match.

Ana folded a sharp crease in the tear-stained letter—not that she had any hope of altering the stark black and white note of command. Oh, to be sure, her uncle had penned an apology for altering the terms of their treaty, explaining that the advantages were so great for both country and family that it was imperative to improvise. He had added that he would not force her into marriage. The decision would be hers.

However, she knew how difficult it was for anyone to stand up to the count—even someone as determined as she was to decide on her own life. Indeed, his last line was an ominous portent for just how intractable his will on this was.

". . . You will thank me for this, bebinka, I have a great deal more experience in life than you do. . ."

Pressing a palm to her forehead, Anna fought to hold back bitter tears. She didn't want to be trapped in a mere match of assets, no matter how convenient it was for her guardian and her government. Indeed, she had become so desperate to escape her uncle's decree that on catching sight of a star before the stormclouds had rolled in, she had found herself wishing for a Christmas miracle. If only she could conjure up a Shakespearean spell, or a *Baba Yaga* from the ancient Russian fairytales to forestall her fate.

What she had gotten was a snowstorm, which, alas, was not going to alter the course of her life, save to delay the inevitable for a few days.

Anna consoled herself with the thought that a courtship could drag on well into the spring. Much could happen during that time, though the start of this particular journey didn't auger well for Luck smiling on her. In the first swirling of snow her coach had become lost, and while it had arrived at this refuge in time to miss the brunt of the storm, her lady's maid had come down with a fever and cough. It had taken most of the evening to see the poor girl settled enough to fall into a fitful sleep.

A glance at the battered clock on the mantel showed it

to be nearly midnight. Only now had she finally been able to slip downstairs and seek a belated supper.

Her lips pursed in a rueful twist. What she needed was a guardian angel to help her soften the strictness of her guardian uncle. But it seemed that even angels were allowed a holiday respite in which to make merry and celebrate good cheer with friends. While she was alone, caught in the midst of a raging storm...

Chin up, Anna told herself. Over the years, she had learned it did little good to give way to disappointment and despair. She had weathered other storms in her life. Somehow she would find her way through this one.

After finishing off the last morsel of apple tart, she gathered her shawl and rose. No doubt her unsettled musing had been exacerbated by fatigue and hunger. In the morning, her situation wouldn't seem quite so bleak. After all, there was an old Russian proverb that said things always looked brighter in the light of a new dawn.

CHAPTER 2

"The snow may not be so deep, but with the ice and frozen ruts, it will be very rough going, milord." The innkeeper eyed the blue skies with an arch of skepticism. "And there is no promise that we have seen the last of the bad weather. If I were you, I wouldn't be in such a rush to be back on the roads."

"No matter," answered Nicholas grimly. "I mean to be on my way within a quarter hour."

"Begging your pardon, sir, but how do you mean to manage that? I thought you said one of your horses was lame."

Nicholas frowned, suspecting he was about to fall victim to highway robbery, as well the vagaries of an English winter. But however outrageous the demand was, money was no object. "I saw another team in the stables," he said.

"Aye. But they're not for hire," replied the innkeeper.

"What do you mean they are not for hire?" Nicholas

pulled a purse from his coat. "Be assured I intend to pay you very well for their use."

"You could offer me a king's ransom in gold, and it still wouldn't change things. They ain't mine to be offering. They belong to the other guest. And there are none others to be had. Not with this weather."

Of all the cursed luck.

"But I simply *must* be in London by Christmas," muttered Nicholas.

The innkeeper lifted his shoulders. "Perhaps your horse will be fit to travel with another day of rest."

Nicholas knew enough about horses to have little faith in such a miracle, even if it was the Christmas season. But seeing there was no point in further argument, he jammed his hands in his pockets and started for the stables. Ye God —as if he didn't have enough to worry about! The way his father had phrased it, the fate of two nations hung in the balance on whether he could make mooncalf eyes at a certain lady on Christmas.

Perhaps there was a chance he could convince his fellow traveler to give up—

WHOMP!

A snowball hit him square in the back of the head. Knocked off balance, his feet flew out from under him and he fell back on his rump.

"Oh, I am terribly sorry, sir! I was just playing a game of fetch with the dog and somehow my aim went dreadfully off."

Nicholas looked around to see an elfin young lady, muffled in furs and high felt boots, cavorting with a terrier in the snow. Despite her words, she did not look a whit contrite. Indeed, she appeared to be biting back laughter.

Scowling, he picked himself up and retrieved his hat. "Hoyden," he muttered, not deigning to dignify her apology with anything more than a frosty nod.

"I beg your pardon?" Twirling a graceful series of spins through the snow, his erstwhile assailant moved toward him. A peek of raven curls had escaped from her ermine-trimmed shako, accentuating the porcelain perfection of her fine-boned features. That a rosy flush suffused her cheeks and a mischievous sparkle lit her sapphire eyes added a bewitching vitality to her beauty.

Nicholas gave himself a rough shake, ostensibly to dislodge the flakes still clinging to his coat. What dark magic had cast its spell over this Christmas? A time of warmth and good cheer was quickly turning into a slippery slide into the depths of Hell.

"You need not bother," he growled, mortified to realize he had been staring like a lackwit for the last few moments. "I don't suppose that a schoolgirl can be expected to behave with any decorum." In truth, he had quickly revised his initial impression, realizing appearances were deceiving—the minx was no mere schoolgirl but rather a stylish young lady.

In no humor to court any further humiliations, he turned on his heel and continued on his way.

His mood suffered a further set-down when a cursory examination of his horse's right fetlock showed the swelling had not gone down. It now appeared his only hope of escaping this debacle was to seek out the fellow who possessed the two glossy chestnuts in the neighboring stalls and try to negotiate a deal. Or, if diplomacy failed, he might just have to resort to groveling in the snow.

Again.

That option appeared even less palatable when Nicholas returned to the taproom and sought out the innkeeper. "Oh, they don't belong to a gentleman, sir," said the man in response to his inquiry. "But rather to a young lady who is traveling alone, save for the company of her servants. . ."

A queasy feeling suddenly came over him.

"Perhaps you caught a glimpse of her outside? She said she wished to have a short stroll before her breakfast." The innkeeper shook his head. "No accounting for the queer taste some folk have. Imagine wanting to walk about in the cold and snow for the fun of it." A thump of the teapot punctuated his inability to fathom the odd quirks of Quality. "As for you, sir, shall I lay out some toast and a plate of shirred eggs and gammon?"

Nicholas made a face. "No, if I am going to have to eat humble pie, I had rather do it on an empty stomach."

THAT HAD KNOCKED a bit of the starch out of the gentleman, thought Anna as she tossed another snowball. The dog barked into delight, and she allowed a burble of laughter to echo the animal's merriment. Lud, he had looked madder than a wet hen at being taken down a peg or two.

Her chin rose a fraction. He had richly deserved the set-down. Perhaps her prank had been a touch childish, yet how dare he accuse her of bad manners when he had been unconscionably rude to the innkeeper, a poor fellow who was doing the best he could.

But then, titled gentlemen were loath to admit to any fault.

She blew out a puff of breath and scooped up another handful of snow. Why was it that most of them were puffed up with a sense of their own importance? They seemed to have no sense of humor or serendipity. That anyone could look so horribly stiff and serious on a magical morning such as this one, when the icicles sparkled like diamonds and the trees looked as if they had been coated in spun sugar—

"Might I have a word with you?"

The snow had muffled the sound of his approach, and as Anna spun around, she nearly lost her footing.

"Forgive me for frightening you." He caught her elbow and she was surprised at the firmness of his grip and the hint of muscle beneath his tailored sleeve.

"Very little frightens me, sir," she said tartly, shaking off his hold. "I assure you, I am not easily intimidated."

He looked at her rather thoughtfully before inclining a small bow. "Then accept my apologies for approaching you without a formal introduction. However, given the pressing circumstances, I hope you will consent to dispensing with the usual formalities of Polite Society."

Having made up her mind to dislike him, Anna responded with deliberate sarcasm. "You act as though a simple snowstorm is cause for grave concern."

"It is."

He was quick with a rejoinder, she gave him that. And oddly enough, his voice was quite pleasant—deep and mellifluous, with none of the affected little mannerisms she so loathed in most Tulips of the *ton*.

"But before I explain," he went on. "Please allow me to introduce myself. I am Nicholas Wrexfax, Lord Killingworth."

Anna couldn't help but note that Lord Killingworth had very nice eyes as well as a pleasant voice. Their jade-green hue had a smoky intensity, and yet there were intriguing sparks of gold flitting beneath the surface.

She looked away quickly, not wanting to see anything good about him.

Still, she could not quite bring herself to be so rude as to snub him completely. "And I am Lady Anna Federova."

"Ah. I imagine that explains why you feel so at home in the wilds of winter." His gaze fell on the lump of snow cradled in her mitten. "I must say, your English is as impeccable as your aim."

Anna bristled. Was he implying that all Russians were uncouth savages? "I should hope so, seeing as my mother was the daughter of the Marquess of Middleton," she retorted, happy to have reason to renew hostilities. "And were they still alive, she and my father would be sadly disappointed if the small fortune they spent on educating me at Mrs. Franklin's Academy for Select Young Ladies had been all for naught."

Lord Killingworth had the grace to flush. "I meant no offense, Lady Anna. I was merely trying to break the ice, so to speak. We did not exactly get off on the right foot during our earlier encounter."

"It was not *I* who slipped and fell on my. . . derriere."

If Nicholas heard her murmured barb, be chose to ignore it. "Might I ask how you came to be stranded in this out-of-the-way place?"

"Most likely in the same way that brought you here. My coachman took the wrong turn." Her lips twitched. "By the by, the stableboy tells me the signpost was knocked askew weeks ago by a stray ram, but no one has bother to fix it."

"Dam. . . drat it." He did not seem to find the news nearly as amusing as she did.

"Come now, it could be much worse," she chided. "The inn may be simple, but it's quite comfortable."

After a small start, he actually smiled, revealing a peek of teeth as white as the surrounding snow. "Then perhaps you would have no objection to spending another night here."

A hint of humor? Anna blinked. That was not the only thing that took her aback. Lord Killingworth was actually very attractive when he was not scowling. His earlier spill had tumbled his carefully combed locks into an unruly shock of gold. The tangle around his ears and collar softened the chiseled cut of his aquiline nose and square jaw. The contrast was intriguing, as if beneath the starched formality and stiff-rumped manners there was still a bit of unfettered spirit eager to break free. His lips seemed to hint at that as well.

They had a most interesting curl. . .

Yes, and his temper had a most atrocious edge, she

reminded herself, quickly averting her eyes. His shout could match that of Uncle Yevgeny, which was certainly not a mark in his favor.

"W-whatever do you mean, sir?" she asked.

"In my experience, a small delay never matters overly much to a young lady," replied Nicholas with a forced heartiness. "While I, on the other hand, have a matter of serious business in London that cannot be put off."

His smile stretched a bit wider. "If you would allow me to continue on with your team, I shall see to it that new horses are sent here from the nearest coaching inn. The inconvenience would be ever so slight, and I would, of course, insist on covering the additional expense."

Anna fixed him with a cold stare. It was just like a haughty, highborn aristocrat to assume his affairs were more important than hers. And that a lady would step aside without a whimper. However, in this case, the gentleman in question had no right to ride roughshod over her.

"Absolutely out of the question." Despite the fact that she was in no hurry to reach her destination, she took a measure of satisfaction in standing her ground. "I, too, have a pressing need to be in Town," she replied, angling her chin in a defiant tilt. "My uncle would be seriously upset if I failed to arrive at the appointed hour."

For a moment, Lord Killingworth looked as though he had been struck dumb.

No doubt he was rarely denied anything. Well, disappointment built character—or so said another Russian proverb. It would do him no harm to cool his heels for a bit. Squaring her shoulders, she prepared to face the expected explosion of gentlemanly ire without giving an inch.

"Forgive me. I had forgotten that it is Christmas," he said quietly. 'Even if it were not a special time, I would not have asked you if my haste were only for personal reasons. It is not, but I shall think of some other way."

His thoughtful response softened her stance. Feeling somewhat childish, she reminded herself that however depressing the holidays were for her, the season was meant to be a time of caring and sharing.

"Well, seeing as it is Christmas, I suppose I could take you along in my carriage until we come to the main road," she responded. "From there you can catch a mail coach to Town."

An instant later she was regretting her spur-of-the-moment offer. The expression of icy hauteur was back on his face, and rather than express appreciation for her Yuletide generosity, Lord Killingworth looked appalled at the idea of having to travel in a public conveyance.

"I suppose I have no choice but to accept," he said grudgingly.

"No, you don't—not unless you wish to walk." Anna gave a toss of her curls, causing the plume of her shako to tickle her cheek. She slapped it away. "Or you could consider strapping blades to your boots and skating to London."

"I could—"

"Or you *could* say thank you, Lord Killingworth."

"I am much obliged, Lady Anna."

Ha! One wouldn't know it by the grim expression on his face.

"However, rather than waste precious time exchanging social niceties," he went on. "Might I point out that it would be prudent to be on the road as soon as possible."

"I am well aware of that, sir. But as my maid was feeling poorly last night, I did not wish to rouse her at first light. Be assured that we will be ready to depart within the hour."

"Thank you," he said, the exaggerated politeness edged with an unmistakable note of mockery.

So much for the prospect of peace on earth and good will toward all men—and women.

Anna gave an inward groan. Yet another overbearing male to make her last little interlude of freedom miserable. This most certainly did *not* promise to be a very merry journey.

Nicholas gave a baleful grimace as he watched Anna march away. Judging by the performance he had just put on, the only diplomatic position to which he could ever aspire was a posting to the outer reaches of Siberia. Polar bears and arctic seals had thick enough hides that his gaffes would merely bounce off them.

As for the elegant young lady...

No doubt she thought him an ass. She had implied as much with her reference to falling on a certain part of his anatomy. He grimaced. To be sure, both his bum and his pride were a bit bruised from the uncharacteristic show of awkwardness. He did not like looking the fool....

A swish of skirts as she paused to pat the dog drew him from his brooding. *Lady Anna Federova.* Like her name, she was an intriguing mix of the familiar and the foreign. She had the creamy complexion of a young English miss, but her blue eyes—their exotic slant accentuated by the pert arch of her raven-dark brows—flickered and danced with a strangely compelling light.

Fire within ice. As if that made any sense.

Nicholas pulled his muffler a bit tighter. He had no business allowing her looks, however alluring, to distract him from his duty, which was getting to London without further delay.

Pulling out his pocketwatch, he grimaced. Immune to the vagaries of weather or women, the minutes were ticking away. He sincerely hoped that unlike many of the pampered young ladies of the ton, Lady Anna did not think it fashionable to keep a man waiting.

He need not have fretted, for, true to her word, the young lady descended from her room well within the allotted time. Nicholas quickly put down his teacup and grabbed his valise. However, the look on her face brought him up short.

"I am afraid my maid has taken a turn for the worse," announced Anna. "She is in no condition to travel."

"You need not worry about the girl receiving proper care, milady," ventured the innkeeper, who had come over to clear the table. "My missus is well known in these parts as a skilled healer. In a few days, I am sure she will be fully recovered."

Anna murmured her thanks, then hesitated. Turning to

Nicholas, she indicated an alcove by the mullioned windows. "Might I have a private word with you, Lord Killingworth?"

The reflections from the snow cast a pattern of light and shadow across her profile as she turned, accentuating the hollowness under her eyes and the pinch of worry around her mouth. She looked very small and very vulnerable standing all by herself. Despite their earlier hostilities Nicholas had to fight off the urge to enfold her in his arms.

"I find myself faced with a very awkward dilemma," she said haltingly, once he had joined her. "I have offered you a ride, sir, but without my maid, it would be terribly improper for us to travel together."

"Of course." He took a moment to swallow his disappointment. "You may think me an ass, Lady Anna, but I assure you I am not a cad. I would never seek to force a lady into risking her reputation."

She lowered her lashes, the thick fringe a dark flutter against her pale cheek. "Now it is my tum to apologize. I did not mean to imply any such thing. Indeed, you. . . you seem a real gentleman."

His mouth crooked up at the corners. "If you wish, I can give you a list of my credentials."

"Are you going to pull out the stud book and read off your pedigree as well?" she asked.

It was not only her snowballs but also her quixotic character that had him strangely off balance. Fire and ice. He sensed that both were used to mask a far more fragile part of herself.

"That was just a jest, sir," she said quickly, before he

could reply. A sigh escaped her lips. "Perhaps an ill-timed one, but I don't suppose you would understand how often we ladies are treated as if we are no different from horses or hounds—well-bred livestock to be sold to the highest bidder." She paused, an unreadable emotion flickering over her features. "At times I cannot help but rail at the unfairness of it."

"When you put it that way, I can see how you would feel angry."

Anna seemed surprised by his statement. "N-not many gentlemen do."

Nicholas reached out and tucked an errant curl behind her ear. She seemed to shiver as his touch grazed her cheek, while he felt a spark of heat tingle on his fingertips. "Far be it for me to add to your discomfort. But I feel I ought to point out that travelling alone, without your maid, will also give rise to unpleasant rumor."

"Yes, I had thought of that, too," confessed Anna. "I seem caught between a rock and a stone."

"I know this will sound self-serving, but the obvious solution is for you to remain here with the girl until she recovers, or until your uncle can send someone else to escort you to Town." After a stretch of silence, he added, "I know how terrible it must seem to think of missing a family Christmas."

She turned, angling her profile even deeper into the shadow. "Like yours, my reasons for returning to Town are not personal. They relate to a matter of important business for my guardian, so I... I cannot delay."

Nicolas didn't miss the tautness in her tone, and though

it was no concern of his, he felt a flare of anger at her uncle. Her earlier outburst made it easy to guess what sort of business she was talking about. So she, too, was being shoved from here to there, as if she were naught but a pawn on a chessboard. The irony of their similar situations would have been rather laughable had not he caught the glimmer of pain in her eyes.

"Then let me think how I can help you." Nicholas rubbed at his chin. "Perhaps the innkeeper knows of a local girl who could be hired to accompany you."

"I—I had not thought of that." She paused a fraction. "What about you, sir? You seemed to imply your presence in Town was of great importance."

"It is, but that isn't your concern. I shall figure out something." Wishing to wipe the pinched look from her face, he essayed a note of humor. "If you would make me one of your snowballs, mayhap I could roll my way to the next coaching stop."

Her lips twitched upward for an instant before her expression once again turned serious. "Perhaps there is another alternative."

"Yes?" encouraged Nicholas.

"That we keep to our original plan. It is not as if any gossip is going to reach Town from here. And if we employ a modicum of discretion, we ought to be able to drop you at the first coaching inn with no one being the wiser." Anna forced a smile. "It would be in keeping with the spirit of the holidays. Surely no harm can come of offering kindness to a stranger."

"The risk does seem small," he mused. "But still, it's not something either of us ought to take lightly."

His note of caution rekindled the fire in her eyes. "Don't you ever wish to shake free of the rules, if only for a fleeting interlude, Lord Killingworth?" she demanded.

"Sorry to disappoint you. If you are looking to encounter a dashing hero on this journey, read Byron's poetry." He had thought himself long past caring about such snide comments about his lack of color. Yet for some reason, her criticism hurt more than he cared to admit.

"With all that expensive education, I would have thought you smart enough to realize that this predicament is nothing to make light of. Surely your instructors taught you that Society does not forgive or forget a mistake, however innocent."

"To hell with Society and all its strictures," she muttered, the angle of her chin defying him to remark on her unladylike language. "If you are afraid of risking your own reputation, I will go on alone. Even if there were a local girl willing to leave her family at Christmas, it would take too long to make arrangements."

"You appear to enjoy courting disaster," he said through gritted teeth. "I cannot in good conscience allow you to continue on your own. But let us pray this lapse in protocol doesn't come back to haunt us."

"Don't be so pessimistic."

"I prefer to think of it as being realistic. In my line of work, I have learned that one can't allow emotion to cloud reason."

"I shudder to think what it is you do," she countered. "Hopefully it does not involve dealing with people."

Stung by her note of scorn, he reacted with equal heat. "For your information, Lady Anna, I am accorded to be *very* skillful in settling quarrels and bringing about a meeting of minds."

"Is that so? Well, it seems you will get a great deal of practice in honing your abilities during the next few hours."

CHAPTER 3

The sun was still shining, but the trip was certainly starting out on a stormy note. Tugging at the cords of her reticule, Anna leaned back against the squabs and listened to the creak of her coachman loading the boot of the coach. Somehow her mood was proving more difficult to untangle. Why could she not simply put Lord Killingworth out of her head?

It was where he belonged—far, far from her most private thoughts and feelings.

He was an oddly infuriating gentleman, arrogant and overbearing one moment, only to show an intriguing glimmer of sensitivity the next.

Don't be a goose, she chided herself. Just because he showed a flash of wit and an attractive smile was no reason to imagine he actually possessed some real depth of character. His own words had warned her not to expect anything out of the ordinary from him.

Several minutes later, His Lordship climbed into the

coach. Without a word, he settled himself in the opposite comer and cracked a book. A surreptitious glance showed it was not Byron, but a thick tome on the history of the Byzantine Empire. No wonder he looked so glum if *that* was the sort of reading he chose for relaxation.

Anna returned to her own book, the latest work by Miss Austen. Her teachers had frowned on such novels for young ladies. And it was no wonder, for with a sharp eye and dry wit, the author masterfully exposed the frailties and foibles of Society. Which was, of course, exactly why Anna found them highly entertaining, even though her laughter was often tempered by a twinge of pain as the observations cut close to home.

The truth hurt at times. She was not so vain as to think her uncle and her acquaintances were the only ones with faults. Like Elizabeth Bennett, she had her own prejudices, and a tendency to be headstrong and highly opinionated. Still, Anna took heart in knowing that she wasn't alone in seeing the absurdities and unfairness in life.

At least with her nose buried in the pages, she felt she was in the presence of a kindred soul.

Until Lord Killingworth's grumble reminded her of another, more unwelcome presence. "Now what is the delay?" he muttered.

"John Coachman is quite thorough in checking that all is in order before setting out," she replied, not looking up from her book. "I imagine he has found some buckle or bolt that needs attending to."

Her amusement over a particularly pithy observation on the page was interrupted by a low snort of air. One that sounded suspiciously like a word that should not have been uttered in front of a lady.

"Really, sir, you have a devil of a temper," she observed without shifting her gaze.

"Me?" His response bristled with indignation. "Ha! I am known for my even disposition."

"Right," she shot back. "You are *always* horribly irritable."

Nicholas drew in a sharp breath. "What makes you say that?"

"To begin with, from the moment you stormed into the inn last night, you have been loud, rude and overbearing, expecting everyone in your path to bow to your needs."

Leather crackled as he shifted uncomfortably on the seat. "I was not aware you overheard my arrival," he said. "I. . . I cannot blame you for thinking me an oaf. The truth is, I haven't been at my best lately."

Surprised at the unexpected frankness, Anna found herself curious. "Is there a reason?"

She half expected him to tell her to mind her own business, but after a stretch of silence, he cleared his throat. "If you must know, I would rather be spending Christmas in the country with my friends, so I am not particularly pleased at having been summoned back to Town."

A sidelong glance showed that his grip on his book was in danger of splitting the spine.

"However," he went on tightly. "When duty calls, I have no choice but to come running like an obedient hound."

"I thought only females were on such a tight leash."

"There is much about the real world that they don't

teach you at Mrs. Franklin's Academy for Select Young Ladies." The note of mockery was directed more at himself than at her. "Gentlemen may appear to have the freedom to roam at will, but trust me, the collar, however subtle, can be just as choking. I—" Nicholas abruptly snapped his book shut. "I shall just have a look at what is holding us up."

Between the jangle of the harness and the whisper of her own conflicted thoughts, Anna could not make out the muffled exchange between Lord Killingworth and her driver. Whatever it was, the discussion did not last long. The arrival of hot bricks and extra blankets finally signaled that they were ready to leave.

"I brought along the last of the meat pie, along with some bread and cheese, in case it takes longer than expected to reach the main road." Nicholas added several oilskin packets to the items the innkeeper had brought out. "It's hardly the sort of fare for a refined young lady, but it will have to do."

"I am not one of those sheltered misses who has never had a taste of life outside of the schoolroom," replied Anna tartly. While she did not want to be thought of as a wild savage, neither did she wish him to view her as just another pampered aristocrat. "I have traveled extensively through Europe and Russia, in far harsher conditions than these, sir, so there is no need to be. . . condescending."

"My apologies." He did not sound overly contrite, and wasted little time in raising his book as a barrier to any further conversation.

She stared at the tooled leather, silently mouthing a rather unladylike word. Lord Killingworth was one of the rare gentlemen she had ever met who had shown a hint of introspection, yet just when the discussion had been taking an interesting direction, he had retreated behind the stiff confines of convention.

Her disappointment was hard to swallow. How she longed to talk about real feelings with a gentleman rather than engage in banal exchanges about the latest fashionable color, or the state of the weather.

Which was, she noticed, threatening to turn as dark as her mood. An ominous line of leaden clouds hovered on the horizon, their gathering force a warning that another storm might be headed their way.

"The sky is now the color of pewter," she pointed out a short while later, unable to concentrate on her reading.

"Do you wish to turn back?" asked Nicholas.

Anna stared out at the fairytale forest, then looked away as her sigh fogged the windowglass. Feeling hemmed in on all sides, she blurted out, "If I had my wish, a Baba Yaga would appear to turn the horses into reindeer and fly the coach to the North Pole."

"Surely it can't be that bad." His scowl softened to a rueful smile. "It would be awfully cold atop the world, not to speak of awfully lonely. There wouldn't be another person around for thousands of miles."

"So much the better," she muttered. "But I doubt you know what it is like to be bound by duty and convention, always at the beck and call of others, with no freedom to make up your own mind. Parents, teachers, guardians— Lud, at times it feels as if even the gardener and the groom may fling orders at me."

Her breath had turned to ice on the window. Slipping off her mitten, Anna traced random patterns through the crystals with her bare finger. "I assure you, there is little difference between me and a mare put up for auction. Neither of us is ever given free rein. Instead, we are expected to submit docilely to spur or whip."

"Gentlemen are not quite as free as you might imagine to run neck and leather through life."

"No?" A bitter note crept into her voice. "Judging from the gossip that flows as freely as champagne at the balls and soirees, I find that hard to believe."

Nicholas did not answer right away, his attention seemingly caught up by his own view out the window. "If it's any consolation, not all English lords are gentlemen of indolent indulgence."

The fact that he did not respond with a lie or a platitude gave her the heart to continue speaking honestly. "No doubt you are once again thinking me childish, Lord Killingworth. Here I am bemoaning what I do not have, rather than counting my blessings." Anna fingered the thick sable trim of her cloak. "Believe me, I am not such a selfish creature as to be unaware of how fortunate I am in life. I have every comfort imaginable. And yet. . ."

Nicholas waited a moment and then murmured, "And yet, not all happiness can be measured in terms of material possessions."

"You. . . you understand." It came out as half question, half statement.

He gave a small smile. "Lady Anna, I have a feeling we are more alike than you think."

The coach was gliding smoothly through the powdery snow, and yet her insides were giving the oddest little lurches, as if they were spinning cartwheels inside her ribcage. Confused, she braced herself against the squabs and sought to shift the conversation to a more even ground.

"I have no parents or siblings with whom to spend Christmas. But you, sir—surely you have a family who shall miss having you there with them to share the joy of opening presents and feasting on roast goose and plum pudding."

"I, too, am an only child," answered Nicolas. "And while my parents are alive and well, there is little these days that draws us together as a family. My mother is quite happy to potter around the family estate in Devonshire, raising her exotic hothouse roses. Indeed, there are times when I wonder whether she cares more about pistils and stamens than she does about flesh and blood." It was said with a smile, but the humor did not quite reach his eyes.

"As for my father. . ." Nicholas exaggerated a wry shrug. "My father does not allow either heavenly or earthly concerns to distract him from his work. Indeed, if the Savior were to be born today in his stables, he would react to the news with a vague frown, then go back to his papers, after admonishing the servants not to disturb him unless something *truly* important had happened."

Anna laughed in spite of everything. "He ought to meet my uncle. It sounds as if the two of them would get along quite well."

"That—or murder each other." Nicholas's chuckle

sounded a rich counterpoint to their amusement. "In my experience, two strong personalities either love or hate each other."

"I have noticed that as well."

"Does your guardian live in London?"

"No. He is just visiting for several months." Hoping to forestall any further personal questions, Anna began thumbing through her book to find where she had left off. "For business."

Nicholas proved to be as persistent as he was perceptive.

"And what sort of business is that?"

"I-I am sorry, but I really can't discuss his affairs," she replied. "They are highly confidential."

"What about the reason he summoned you back to Town?"

"I would rather not discuss that either, if you please. It is. . . very personal."

"And obviously very painful." Nicholas accepted the rebuff without argument. "You have my sympathy." He paused. "Seeing as I, too, am traveling under duress, perhaps the less said about the subject the better. Shall we make a pact not to press each other on our respective reasons for the duration of the journey?"

Grateful for the suggestion, Anna was quick to reply. "You will not find your skills at negotiating tested in this case. I gladly agree."

"Then I will return to the world of Byzantine politics," he said, holding up his book. "Whatever your uncle is involved in, it could not possibly rival the Greeks and the Turks for cunning or intrigue."

Ha! Anna almost laughed aloud, but managed to clear her throat with a cough instead. "Before you do, I have yet another apology to make. I was not only very rude earlier with my remarks on your temper and your skills at dealing with people, but also very wrong. You are very good at putting a person at ease."

"It is already forgotten," he murmured. "As you witnessed last night, I am all too aware of how easy it is to suffer a lapse in judgment when one is upset." He glanced at her book before turning a page of his own volume. "I take a bit of solace from the fact that some of Miss Austen's characters behave even more foolishly than we have."

They settled into a companionable silence. Cozy beneath the soft folds of her thick merino blanket Anna picked up the thread of the story, and noted that on paper, closer scrutiny of the individuals involved did not always magnify their foibles.

THE SOUND WAS DECEPTIVELY MILD, a soft flutter, something akin to the beating of a moth's wings against the glass windowpanes. Nicholas pulled back the drapery only to find the view was of naught but vague shapes obscured by swirling snow. A gust of wind rattled the door.

"It looks to be getting worse," he said.

Anna yawned and stretched her legs. "I wonder how much farther we have to go. It feels as if we have been travelling for hours."

"I fear the miles have not rolled by as quickly as the minutes. If we—"

A cracking lurch cut off his words and sent Nicholas skidding across the smooth leather. As the sound of splintering wood exploded in his ears, the coach rocked back, flinging him up into the air where he hovered for an instant before landing in Anna's lap.

"Hell's Bells!" His curse echoed the cacophony of confusion outside. As he struggled to untangle his limbs from the twist of blankets and clothing, the wind whipped pellets of ice against the windows and the horses set up another chorus of frightened whinnies. From his box, the coachman cried for help.

To her credit, Anna did not panic. She wriggled out from under him and set to freeing his boot from her knotted skirts.

Brave girl, he noted, though aloud he snapped only a brusque "Stay here" as he dove for the door and wrenched it open. Fighting his way through the driving snow, Nicholas caught the driver as he fell from his icy perch.

"T-T-Tree fell across the way." Blue with cold, the man's lips were having difficulty forming distinct words. "M-Managed to steer the team clear b-but I fear the w-wheel..."

Nicholas saw that the wheel was trapped by the broken branches of a large spruce. He took hold of one of the shattered stumps, but abandoned the effort after several heaves proved there was no way he was going to dislodge it on his own.

"If we back the coach up," he yelled above the howl of

the storm, "I think we can manage to pull the wreckage free."

"Aye, sir." The coachman made a game try at returning to his seat, but his awkward fumblings quickly made it clear that his wrist had been injured in the accident.

"I had better take charge," said Nicolas. "It will take two good hands to control the team."

The man winced. "Aye, but it will also take at least that to clear the branches."

Nicholas took a moment to assess the options—which, he decided, were extremely limited. "We will have to make a try at it. There is no other choice—"

"Actually there is, sir." Anna materialized out of the wind-whipped flakes, a muffler wound up to the tip of her nose, its ends tied over her hat to snug it in place. "Let me handle the ribbons, while you help John."

"Too dangerous," he replied gruffly. "Go back inside."

"*Balvan*! I have a great deal of experience in driving a coach in these conditions."

"Did you just call me a horse's arse in Russian?" he demanded, stifling the urge to laugh.

"Yes—but if you wish to ring another peal over my head for hoydenish behavior, I suggest you do it later," shot back Anna.

"She is a dab hand on the box, sir," volunteered the coachman. "I can attest to her skill."

As a frigid gust nearly swept him off his feet, Nicholas gave a grim nod. "Very well. We won't stand on ceremony." After directing the two others to take up their places, he maneuvered the skittish animals into position to straighten the coach. "Ready?"

Anna tightened her grip on the reins.

"NOW!"

After a few slippery moments, the horses responded to the tugs and shouts, their hooves digging into the fast-drifting snow. The coach inched back, slowly but surely, until they were able to extricate the trapped wheel. Though several spokes were cracked and the rim bent, it looked as if it would hold up for a few more miles.

The same could not be said for the coachman, who was trying to mask his pain with a thin smile. Ignoring the man's weak attempt at argument, Nicholas bundled him inside the coach and tipped a flask of brandy to his iced lips. It was a moment or two before he realized he had left Anna to fend for herself.

"May the devil's arse be buried in ice," he swore, reaching for the door latch.

It snapped open with no help from him.

"Ha—Hell just might freeze over in this weather." Anna sounded almost cheerful as she scrambled in and slapped the snow from her mittens. "I trust you have saved a sip for me."

Thick flakes clung to her fur hat and ice rimmed her dark lashes, giving her the look of a storm-tossed ermine. A very adorable storm-tossed ermine. *And a very brave one.* Of all the young ladies he knew, Nicholas couldn't think of a one who wouldn't have swooned in fright by now. While Lady Anna seemed about to succumb to. . .

Laughter?

It was a sweetly musical sound that seemed to lighten the confined space with a note of sunshine. Nicholas found himself smiling in spite of the circumstances.

"Well done," he murmured, passing over the brandy. "I would never have imagined a highborn lady could take hold of adversity like that."

"And I would never have imagined a proper gentleman could carry his own weight," she retorted, but with a twinkle in her eye. "And if you are about to remark that a highborn lady ought not imbibe in anything stronger than ratafia punch, you may bite your tongue."

"If I could, I would be offering you champagne," he murmured. Strangely enough, he found he was developing a taste for her effervescent spirit, however unconventional. In comparison, every other young lady he knew suddenly seemed flat.

Anna took a tiny taste of the brandy, then handed it back. "Actually, I would prefer vodka," she murmured.

"I shall ring for one of the footmen and ask him to fetch a bottle. Along with a crystal bowl full of caviar."

Another laugh. He was sorry to hear it die away more quickly than the first one.

Her expression turned serious as she rooted around in one of the storage compartments and drew out a length of linen. "Let me have your hand, John. That wrist needs to be bandaged."

"But milady, you ought not have to tend to me—"

"Don't be foolish." She already had hold of his sleeve and was folding back the cuff. "This should help stave off any further swelling." Her gaze angled up, looking for

Nicholas's eyes. "However, you won't be in any condition to drive."

"As to that," he replied. "I will take his place on the box."

"And I will spell you," she added firmly.

Before he could argue, the coachman voiced his own reservation. "Sir, with the wheel as weak as it is, it might not be wise to risk pushing on. The snow and ice has become awfully treacherous on this narrow road. Another accident might turn out to be far more serious than the one we just escaped."

Nicholas frowned. "What are you suggesting?"

"That I go ahead on foot and fetch help. We have traveled some distance, and by the innkeeper's direction, the next village cannot be far off."

"Out of the question," exclaimed Anna. "I'll not have you run such a risk."

"The storm is letting up," replied the coachman, pointing out a sliver of blue in the slate gray clouds. "And there is nothing wrong with my legs, milady. The way is clear enough that I am in no danger of getting lost. I should be back in a short while with a safer vehicle. If I am not, then his lordship can attempt the drive."

"He has a point," mused Nicholas. A more prolonged look out the window showed that the snow had stopped and the dark clouds appeared to be blowing off to the east. "All things considered, the plan is a prudent one."

"There must be another way," she protested.

"If you have a better proposal, I am willing to hear it."

Her lips parted, but remained frozen in silence.

Nicholas began assembling some essentials for the

coachman to take with him. "Lady Anna, like it or not, we must be. . ."

"Practical." Her sigh blunted the edge of irony.

"Sometimes, discretion is the better part of valor," he murmured, adding a pair of extra mittens from his valise and the muffler from his neck to the packet of food in the other man's hand. "Your courage and concern are commendable, but pushing onward might only end up being far more dangerous for all concerned."

She signaled her surrender with a small nod.

"That goes for you, too," he was forced to add as the coachman tried to refuse the food and clothing. "Now be off with you. Stick to the road, and if you encounter any difficulty, do not hesitate to turn back."

After looping the length of merino wool up over his ears, the man snapped off a brisk salute and slipped out into the cold.

"Do you always remain so calm and unrattled in the face of an emergency?" asked Anna as the door fell shut.

"Being a stick in the mud has its advantages—it takes a great deal to make me budge."

She colored. "Oh, dear! Must you remind me of all the regrettable things I have uttered over the course of this day?"

To keep such a becoming shade of pink upon her cheeks, he would consider repeating their conversations word for word. In Latin and Greek, if need be.

"You no doubt look on me as a hopeless hoyden," she said softly. "Now that I have shown my true colors."

"I do not see you in quite so harsh a light, Lady Anna."

She shied back from the window as the sun scudded out from behind the clouds. In a moment it was gone again, dimming the uncertainty in her eyes.

What inner turmoil drove her to seek refuge in shadow? Nicholas had an inkling he knew its cause, which seemed confirmed by her troubled reply.

"Then you are the rare exception. Most gentlemen expect a lady to resemble bleached muslin—soft, pliable, and leached of all texture and hue." Abruptly changing position, she leaned back to face the panes of glass and cupped her chin in her hand. "I have always loved winter, and the way the world appears after a snowfall. The pristine white blanket is so pure, so perfect. It covers a multitude of flaws, hides the imperfections, softens the jagged edges...."

Her voice trailed off as she stared at the pale trees. "Everything looks so hopeful and full of promise, as if life itself were a blank canvas, on which one could start afresh."

"And then it melts away," mused Nicholas.

"Yes, I know." Her voice was sad, subdued. "It's only an illusion."

He thought for a long moment. "In many ways, what you are speaking about is really the true spirit of Christmas. It seems to me that it is a time to remind ourselves that there is always hope, always a chance for the rebirth of light and laughter, no matter that the days are at their darkest."

"Why, Lord Killingworth," she whispered after a moment. "You are a very wise man."

He smiled. "Sorry, I have no frankincense, gold or

myrrh to offer you, just a piece of rather moldy cheddar." From within another square of oilskin he produced half a loaf of dark bread. Cutting off a slice, he topped it off with a crumble of the cheese and presented it to her with a flourish. "Along with a crust of stale rye."

Her mouth quivered, then slowly curled up at the corners. "I think it quite the most lovely Christmas gift I have received since... since I was a child."

Nicholas was too well attuned to the nuances of language to miss her last minute change of words. A shapely figure was not the only thing hidden beneath the fur-trimmed coat. *Secrets.* She had secrets too personal, too painful to share.

Ah, but didn't everyone? he thought, uncomfortably aware of his own inner conflicts, and how carefully he tried to keep them under wraps.

Lud, what a pair they made—two prickly strangers, forced to travel by the call of duty, and suddenly thrown together by chance. Her problems were not really any of his concern, and yet he felt an inexplicable bond had formed between them.

Trying to lighten her bleak mood, he kept up his light banter. "What! You mean to say a porcelain doll can hold a candle to this exquisite delicacy?"

"It was a rocking horse, painted bright yellow, with a flaxen mane and tail soft as spun silk." Anna shivered as she nibbled at the morsel of food. "I used to imagine I could ride to the moon and back if I wished to." A sigh. "But like all childish fantasies, such dreams soon came crashing back down to earth."

Sympathy only seemed to be making things worse.

He tried another strategy. "And here I was thinking you had more bottom than most highborn young ladies. But I see I was wrong. A tumble or two, and you run for cover, feeling egregiously sorry for yourself."

Her eyes blazed, just as he had hoped, burning away the look of dull despair. "That's most unfair, sir!" she exclaimed. "Why, I have faced plenty of hardships that would send any of your cosseted female friends into a paroxysm of. . ." Anna's indignation trailed off as she caught sight of his twitching lips. "Wretch—you were trying to make me angry."

"I would rather hear fire in your voice than such a note of defeat," he admitted. "Trust me, we all experience times when our dreams soar a bit higher than reality allows."

"Even you?"

"Yes, even me. The fall back down to earth may leave a few bruises, but the trick is to dust yourself off and get back on your horse."

She nibbled at the last bit of cheese while digesting his last words. "I don't imagine it happens often. Gentlemen are so rarely knocked from the saddle."

"You saw me land flat on my. . . bum. A rather lowering experience, I might add, that put several distinct black-and-blue marks on my pride."

"At the time, you appeared to need a set-down. But I was wrong, and owe you yet another apology." Her gaze dropped. "My judgment seems greatly askew these days."

"But not your aim," pointed out Nicholas.

She didn't smile. "That is hardly a mark in my favor."

"On the contrary," he replied. "I think it quite admirable that a young lady possess practical skills, and the spirit to use them."

Anna cast him a doubtful look. "You are teasing me again, I expect."

"No, I'm not. You're right to say that in many ways, young ladies of the ton are indistinguishable from one another. In a ballroom, they do have a tendency to blend together into one blur of pastel silks. A very pretty blur, to be sure."

His lips quirked. "However, up close, pastels tend to look a trifle insipid. I often find myself wishing for some sort of show of real color."

Nicholas watched as her eyes deepened to an indescribably unique shade of blue. Deep, mysterious, and rippled with subtle shadings ranging from turquoise to indigo.

A man could drown in such a hue. And die happily.

"Even if that show of color takes the form of a snowball smack to the back of your head?" she asked.

He found himself grinning. "You certainly leave a lasting impression, Lady Anna. A number of gentlemen might not like it that you have strong opinions, as well as a strong arm. But you also have pluck and courage. I cannot think of another lady with whom I would rather be trapped in the wilds."

His observation stirred an unfathomable reaction. It was gone in the blink of an eye as she lowered her lashes. "That's nice of you to say, sir. Most of the time, I hear only florid compliments on my looks or shameless flattery of my mediocre skills on the pianoforte."

"And you do not like that?"

"No. In truth it is very wearisome."

Anna made no protest as he tucked another blanket over her lap and settled her head on his shoulder. "Try to get a bit of sleep, then. There will still be a long way to go once your coachman returns."

"Perhaps you could come on with us to London after all," she murmured into the folds of his coat.

Dangerous. That road could only lead to trouble.

"It's probably best that we go our separate ways," he replied softly.

*I*n her dream, she was being chased by a big black bear whose gaping jaws stretched into an uncanny resemblance of her uncle's smile. *Snap. Snap.* The teeth were coming ever closer, threatening to swallow her into a maw of darkness.

Shrinking back with a small cry, Anna found herself sheltered inside something reassuringly warm and solid. Her lashes fluttered and she was vaguely aware of a dark shape swooping in to ward off the danger.

"No need to be alarmed." Nicholas brushed another tangled curl from her cheek. "The howl is just the sound of the wind picking up."

Now fully awake, Anna sat up. "How long have we been sitting here? It looks dark as midnight outside."

"Not more than an hour, but I am afraid the storm has come back with a vengeance." The wood paneling shivered as another gust slammed into the coach. "I don't think we can expect a rescue party anytime soon. We are going to have to fend for ourselves."

Even with her nose pressed up against the glass, she could make out naught but an impenetrable white shroud surrounding them. "Lud, the temperature is dropping as well. If it gets much colder, we will have to consider abandoning the vehicle and digging a snow cave."

"A snow cave?"

"In Russia, it is a common practice when travelers are stranded in a storm. The snow provides much more insulation than a drafty vehicle. It is actually quite cozy, and can make the difference between life and death."

"How very interesting." She had half expected Nicholas to dismiss the idea as far too outlandish, but he looked rather intrigued. "Do you speak from experience?"

No doubt it would only add to her image of being a very foreign, outlandish sort of person. But she had grown accustomed at school to being considered different from the other girls.

"Yes." Her chin rose a touch, as if to deflect any derision. "My grandmother and I were caught in a wild snowstorm while traveling from Moscow to her country estate in Obuchovo. I was only fourteen and a bit frightened, but she had braved many a winter and made it seem like a grand adventure." Her tone turned slightly wistful. "She kept me entertained through the night by recounting traditional Russian folk tales, with their fearless *bogatyrs*, enchanted ice maidens and magical firebirds. I was disappointed come morning, when a search party found us and dug out our sleigh."

"I can well imagine," said Nicholas, his voice seeming to echo the same note of wistfulness as her own. "*The Feather of Finist the Falcon* was a particular favorite of mine when I was a schoolboy."

"You are familiar with Russian wonder tales?" she asked in surprise.

"I usually had my nose buried in a book while the other lads were out playing cricket." He made a wry face. "You are not the first one who has thought me a stick in the mud."

Wishing that her tongue had not been so well aimed as her snowball, Anna said as much.

"No need for remorse," came the cheerful reply. "Such boring habits came in quite handy when I met up with a partisan band in Portugal."

"Y-You were in Portugal," her eyes widened. "With the partisans?"

"Just for a short time. I was delegated to make a rather minor delivery to one of the less important chieftains. Luckily for me, I had read an arcane Moorish text on mountain warfare, for when we were set upon by a regiment of French dragoons. . ." Nicholas went on to tell a pithy anecdote that Anna suspected did not give near enough credit to his actions in fighting off the enemy.

She was thinking on how to respond when a jangling of the harness rang out above the din of the storm. "Lud, I have forgotten the poor horses!" she exclaimed. "In Russia, the sleighs carry horse blankets for just such an emergency. Unless the storm abates. . ." Wiping the frozen vapor from the windowpane, she tried to peer outside.

Nicholas was already buttoning up his coat. "I saw a small stand of pine trees close by. They should provide an excellent shelter from the snow and wind."

"Lord Killingworth, wait! I should like to come help."

"And turn into a frozen Snow Queen?" He paused with his hand on the latch. "I much prefer you as a flesh-and-blood young lady. So please, do me the great favor of staying here for the moment."

Her pulse suddenly quickened with a rush of heat. Which made no sense, seeing as ice crystals clung to her coat and mittens. "Well, then," she stammered. "Please do be careful."

A flurry of snow nearly obscured his grin. "Don't worry. I have no desire to transform from a stick in the mud to an icicle in the snow."

The horses were soon sheltered, and as it turned out, the wind died down right after Nicholas returned. So it wasn't necessary to go the extreme of seeking refuge in the drifts that had all but buried the coach wheels.

Layered atop the fur carriage throw, the extra blankets ensured that her makeshift bed was quite comfortable. Anna wiggled her toes, finding she could almost stretch out full-length on the narrow bench. While on the facing seat, Lord Killingworth must be feeling like a *matryoshka* doll with his limbs crammed tightly into a confined space. He had refused all but one thin covering, and must have been half frozen as well.

After a restless few minutes, guilt weighed too heavily on her for sleep to come. Sitting up, she was about to insist he take one of her blankets when a soft yet unmistakable buzzing stilled her lips.

The man was snoring. It was an oddly intimate sound. And strangely comforting. Anna lay back and stared up into the darkness. Come to think of it, a great many things about Lord Killingworth were surprisingly reassuring. Far from being an arrogant prig, he had shown himself to be thoughtful, well read and funny. And at the first sign of trouble, he had assumed command with a cool calmness that had saved them from further injury.

She blinked, aware that she had slowly come to see him —and herself—in a whole new light, though its flicker still left much in shadow. It had been some years since she had taken any real joy in Christmas, but now, this chance encounter with a stranger had made her feel a little less alone in the world. The gift—however small, however fleeting—kindled a tiny flame of hope that she might once again share a feeling of closeness, of kinship with another person.

Listening to the slow, steady rhythm of his slumber, she was soon lulled into a peaceful sleep.

It was the resinous curl of wood smoke that tickled her senses back to consciousness. Throwing off her covers, Anna quickly tugged on her coat and boots. Her hairpins, however, proved a more daunting challenge. She didn't dare glance at herself in the windowpane, sure she would look a fright.

"Good morning," said Nicholas as she climbed down from the coach. He had cleared a small patch of ground to the bare earth and was fanning a spark from his flint and steel to life. "Do you always sleep so soundly?"

"Only when I stay awake half the night listening to a strange gentleman's snores."

"I should have warned you." He didn't look around. "Several of my friends have likened it to a dull saw cutting through the keel of a forty-gun frigate."

It was another point in his favor that he could make fun of himself. And the score inched a notch higher as he turned in profile, the snow reflecting a dappling of silvery light across his chiseled features.

"It wasn't quite that bad." Anna watched him strip off his gloves and carefully arrange the thin curls of wood into a small pyramid. A great many gentlemen of her acquaintance were quick to boast of their skills at shooting or dancing or choosing the cut of a waistcoat, but she could not recall one admitting to knowing how to fix an axle or coax a fire from damp shavings of wood. But by now, she was not at all surprised that he did not kick up a dust about getting his hands dirty.

"You do not seem to mind doing menial tasks," she observed.

"Not when it is necessary." He dusted his palms, then picked up the knife and began cutting more fuel for the fire. "I would rather shed my dignity than my life."

"Ever practical, sir?"

"Practical, prudent and pragmatic," he agreed. "I warned you not to expect Lord Byron's Corsair hero as your companion on this journey."

He *did* look very raffish with his uncombed locks

grazing his rumpled linen and a gleam of golden whiskers stubbling his jaw. Trying to put such thoughts out of her mind, Anna stood up and hugged her arms to her chest. "Speaking of journeys, we should probably be harnessing the horses and starting off."

Nicholas threaded a morsel of bread onto a sharpened stick and held it over the meager flames. "I am afraid we are not going anywhere." Seeing her surprised expression, he waggled the piece of toast at the snowy silhouette of their coach. "I checked earlier on the wheel, and what with the weight of the ice and snow, the damaged spoke had cracked clean through."

"We could ride on to the next inn," suggested Anna.

"Too dangerous." The bread angled heavenward. "With the clouds as thick as they are, I won't chance it." After one last pass over the coals, he held the stick at arm's length. "Have some breakfast. It's hardly a mouthful, but we had better conserve what we have."

A nibble of the toasted crust caused her to cough.

He plucked a tin cup from the coals. "Sorry, unlike the wizard in *The Frog Prince*, I am not able to conjure up a spell to turn frozen apples into a pot of steaming tea."

"This is magical enough, sir." Anna sipped at the cider, feeling an extra warmth tingling through her limbs. Lord Killingworth had a most delicious sense of humor—dry and spiced with a whimsical irony. As she swirled the last dregs, she felt an odd sort of emptiness in the pit of her stomach.

Strong. Capable. Modest. Adding on a number of his other attributes, Anna realized she had never savored a gentleman's company quite so much. Yet quite likely their paths would never cross again after this interlude.

Her fingers tightened around the cup, suddenly feeling chilled to the bone.

"Your cheeks are looking pale as ice, Lady Anna," he said quietly. "We had best not linger here too long, exposed to the elements, lest you succumb to frostbite."

It was her heart, she feared, not her face, which was in danger of suffering some irreparable damage. The cold had seeped straight to her core. Not that she could quite explain why. Lord Killingworth would probably have some insight to offer on chance and fate. But she felt awkward, unsure.

Unsure of what, she asked herself. Of whether he would laugh if she told him her thoughts? Of whether she would cry?

Better to keep silent than risk breaking the fragile camaraderie that had formed between them.

Eyeing her with growing concern, Nicholas tucked the blanket more snugly around her shoulders. "I had a look around while you were sleeping. The ruins of an old abbey are not too far off. The walls are crumbling, but there is a roof overhead and room to move about. If we bring along the blankets and a few essentials, I daresay it will be a bit more comfortable place to wait out the weather than a cramped, drafty coach." He paused. "That is, if you are feeling up to the trek."

She nodded. "Of course. It is a sensible move to take leave of the coach."

· · ·

AFTER STRAPPING their luggage atop one of the horses, Nicholas turned to the other animal and arranged a blanket in place as a saddle. "Let me give you a hand up." Worried about her pallor, he tried to tease a bit of color back to her face. "You show a very pretty ankle, Lady Anna," he murmured, as he laced his gloves beneath her boot.

"Lord Killingworth, my leg is presently covered by something resembling a small furry animal."

"Yes, but were it not, I'm sure it would be a most delightful sight."

"How *very* improper of you to say so."

Her burble of amusement encouraged him to go on. "Yes, well, considering our present predicament, I think we can safely say that propriety has long since flown out the window. Let us hope our necks have not gone with it."

He meant it as a joke, but the smile froze on her face. "If you are worried that you are going to find yourself ensnared by the circumstances, don't be. I promised that you would suffer no consequences because of this journey. Your reputation shall remain unsullied." If anything, her voice turned colder. "And your leg unshackled, if that is what is bothering you."

Hell's teeth. What perfidious fairy dust had been mixed in with the snow? In the past, he had always maintained a rigid correctness in any conversation with a lady. But Anna had made him feel at ease. As if he might be himself.

Ha. And pigs might fly.

"That was not what I meant at all," replied Nicholas. "I was merely. . ." Frustrated, he kicked at the snow. "To the devil with reputations and rules! Would that I could shake off all the dratted chains of convention."

A powdering of flakes shot up, sparkling like jewels in the peekaboo sunlight. So, too, did the first notes of laughter lighten the air. The sound grew richer, and more brilliant as it caught in the breeze.

"Why, sir! If you raised your voice an octave, you would sound exactly like me! However, as you wear boots and breeches instead of silks and satins, it is termed 'letting off steam' rather than 'falling in a fit of vapors.' But call it what you will, would you like the loan of my vinaigrette?" Anna gave a small shake of her reticule. "I am sure it is in here somewhere."

His shoulders stiffened, and then he caught a glint of the merriment in her eyes. "Minx! Are you. . ."

"Teasing you?" Her peal of laughter rang delightfully musical to his ear. "Yes, I suppose I am. I have never dared do so with a gentleman before, but when you let yourself unbend, you are. . . different. So do not turn too starchy, Lord Killingworth."

"Do not turn too saucy, Lady Anna."

She stuck out her tongue. "What is good for the goose is good for the gander."

Grinning, he made a last check of the luggage and took up the reins. *Different.* It was a start in the right direction. Though where it would lead, he could not hazard a guess.

"Let us hope we do not end up burned to a crisp, " he murmured.

They set off through the windblown snow, and for a time both of them seemed content to let their thoughts drift, like the swirl of flakes kicked up by the horses. As he trudged through the knee-deep powder, Nicholas found himself simply enjoying the soft sounds of a winter's morning. The muffled swoosh of his steps. . . the stirring of the snow-coated pine boughs. . . the musical tinkle of the brass harness fittings, which sounded a little like faraway church bells. It was peaceful. It was. . .

It was Christmas! Or nearly so.

"Good Lord!" His exclamation formed a whispery cloud around his lips. "Tonight is Christmas Eve. The holiday festivities will have to go on without us, for it goes without saying that we will never make it to Town in time for our engagements."

He angled a look over his shoulder. "I hope that is not too bitter a disappointment."

Anna's eyes were downcast. "In truth, I did not feel much like celebrating."

"Come, if you were in Spain, your eyes would be all aglitter on this eve as you wrapped sweetmeats in gold foil." Wishing to lighten the look on her face, he said the first fanciful thing that popped into his head. "It is a tradition that all unmarried young ladies of the land prepare treats for the elfin folk who fly in on storks to leave a gift on the pillow of every sleeping child."

Her lashes lifted ever so slightly. "How do they get into the houses?"

"They, er, fly down the chimneys." A gust whistled through the trees. "While in Denmark, the celebration takes on a different form. The North Wind blows in through the cracks in the windows and leaves an ice crystal on the mantel for every member of the family. When the morning comes, the fire is kindled to a great flame and the frozen gift melts into a wish."

Anna's gaze had regained a bit of sparkle. "In Russia, a Baba Yaga is said to fly in on a mortar and pestle, leaving gifts for those who have been good all year and lumps of coal for those who have been bad."

"Ah, that is nothing compared to the monkeys of Malta, who according to an old Templar rite are allowed to pelt miscreants with rotten oranges from dawn to dusk on Christmas day."

A burble of laughter cut off any further fantasies. "Really, sir, how do you come up with such outrageous bouncers at the drop of a hat?"

"As a government official, I am expected to be creative with language."

"You mean to lie through your teeth?" she demanded.

He managed to assume an expression of mock indignation but it quickly quirked into a grin. "Well, if you put it that way..."

"You have a wonderfully whimsical imagination, Lord Killingworth," she said softly. "Thank you for lifting my spirits. I know everyone is expected to be happy at Christmas. But I find it... hard."

"If you are thinking that something is missing, Lady Anna, you are not alone." Nicholas cut around an outcropping of rock. "No doubt it sounds blasphemous, but the season has always left me cold. There is so much jolliness all around—the cheerful laughter, the festive decorations of evergreen and mistletoe, the smells of sugar and spice perfuming the air. One feels guilty about not getting into the spirit of things. And yet, so much of the celebrating feels forced, or superficial. It sometimes seems the true meaning of the holiday has been lost."

"I hate Christmas," she blurted out.

Nicholas halted, ostensibly to give the horses a rest. "May I ask why?" he said, his hand lingering on her knee after he had smoothed out the folds of her coat.

"Because it used to be a magical time of light." She sniffed. "And love."

"What happened to change that?"

Anna hesitated before answering. "I was in school here in England. My parents had been called away to St. Petersburg, but they had promised to return in time for us to share the holidays together, as we always did. However, the passage through the Baltic was a rough one, and by the time their ship reached Antwerp, it was running several days late."

She swallowed hard. "They should never have set sail that night, but the harbormaster said my father was so anxious to reach Dover without further delay that the captain relented. A winter gale. . ." Her voice, which had grown brittle as ice, finally cracked.

His hand found hers and clasped it tightly. Through the thick wool he could feel her fingers. They were clenched together, as if seeking solace from each other. "If your uncle were here, I would hit him with a thumping right cross, rather than a snowball. He must be as hard and unfeeling as a lump of coal to have you traveling on your own so close to Christmas."

"He is not uncaring, merely unaware. At the time, he was away in the Far East. I don't think he ever knew the exact date of the shipwreck. Or if he did, the significance did not quite sink in. You see, he is of the Orthodox faith, as are most Russians. By their calendar, Christmas comes in early January." Her lips quivered. "In any case, he is too busy ordering important affairs to think about such small tragedies."

Without saying a thing, Nicholas pulled her down from the makeshift saddle and into his arms. He sensed she did not need words, just the unspoken warmth of a heartfelt hug.

Ice crackled in the branches overhead. From a nearby stump, a solitary raven flapped up into the sky. Finally, at the sound of a frosty snort from one of the horses, Anna lifted her cheek from his collar with an answering sigh. "You are immensely kind to offer a shoulder to lean on, Lord Killingworth. Though I fear with all my sniffling I've left your linen rather wilted."

"We both agreed it was better not to be too starchy," he said. "And I would much rather you call me Nicholas."

" Very well. . . Nicholas." Blinking away a last tear, she straightened her fur hat. "We cannot stand in one place forever. The horses are growing chilled. We really must move on."

Though loath to let her go, Nicholas let her pull away. His gaze moved across the snow-covered pastureland to where the ruins of the abbey were just visible above the crest of a hill. "Would that I could make the journey an easier one for you."

Like her, he was speaking of more than mere physical distance.

"I'm not sure how far I could have come without you," she murmured as he helped her back onto her horse.

"Tell me," he said, once they had gotten under way again. "What are the things you recollect most about Christmas with your family?"

"Lud, I have a myriad of marvelous memories." Anna thought for a moment, a wistful smile curling the corners of her mouth. "I recall how Papa would search the woods for the biggest Yule log he could find. How Mama delighted in playing Christmas carols on the pianoforte—from English to Russian, and a whole mix of languages in between."

A pause. "How she would have Cook decorate the dining table with cherubic angels carved out of ice, their chubby little arms filled with candles and sugared plums."

"It sounds truly wonderful."

Looking as though she did not quite trust her voice, Anna nodded.

He let the conversation trail off into the rhythmic crunch of snow. As the abbey walls came into sharper focus, an idea began to take form in his head. A crazy one to be sure, seeing as they were stranded in the wilds, with barely a crust of bread and bit of cheese between them.

But miracles could happen, Nicholas reminded himself, if one believed them possible. To go along with the cherished memories of Christmas past, he was determined to make the advent of Christmas this year an evening that Anna would not forget.

CHAPTER 5

agic. Her wish upon a star must have bounced off Antares, gathered momentum as it circled Polaris and finally reached the ear of some powerful wizard or warlock. For nothing short of unearthly enchantment could explain the sight that now greeted her gaze.

Eyes wide with wonder, Anna looked around the remains of the ancient chapel. Barely half an hour ago it had been a dark, damp space, with wind whistling through the crumbling mortar, dead leaves and mouse droppings that had covered the worn stone floor.

And now?

Fatigue and hunger did strange things to the brain, and she was awfully tired and hungry. That, of course, had not stopped her from demanding to help make their temporary shelter habitable. So when Nicholas had asked if she would chip through the ice of a nearby stream while he gathered kindling, she had gladly taken up the old bucket they had found and stumbled off.

Setting down her load, she pressed an icy mitten to her brow, wondering if she was dreaming. But no, a peek through the wool showed that the vision was still there. In the far corner a blaze of merry flames danced up from a massive log whose rotund girth matched that of a brandy cask. Above it, a garland of evergreen branches festooned the entire length of the weathered wall, its needles perfuming the air with the fragrance of fresh-cut pine.

Her breath then caught in her throat as she spied a flickering of light set off from the main fire.

"It's not quite finished." Knotting a strip of linen around a twig of white birch, Nicholas smeared the cloth with sticky pine resin and added it to the other wooden candles he had fashioned. It burst into flame, illuminating the blocks of ice he had hollowed out to hold the display. "They are not the most elegant tapers, and my skills as a sculptor leave something to be desired, but—"

"They are beautiful," she whispered. "Simply beautiful."

"Come, let us make the last few ones together."

Anna sat down on the blanket and took up a remnant of cloth. "How did you ever manage the Yule log?" she asked.

"With the help of the horses. I rigged a length of the reins as a crude sling."

"You. . ." A shower of sparks shot up as she lit her candle from one of his. "You have worked miracles, Nicholas."

"Abracadabra!" Making a wry face, he waved a branch at the burning log. "Now if only I could make a Christmas goose appear for a holiday repast."

The fluttering in her stomach had nothing to do with hunger. Not for fowl. Or fish, for that matter.

Lud, she could feast on his smile alone and never feel an emptiness inside her again.

"I fear it will be the same sorry supper of bread and cheese—save for one small treat." With a flourish, he produced a tin of tea from his coat pocket. "I found this in my valise. In my haste to take leave of my friends, I forgot to leave behind the special blend of Oolong that William requested from Town."

"Any more magic up your sleeve?"

He made a show of looking up his cuffs. "I'm afraid that's all for now. I shall just kindle a very ordinary fire for cooking, and use our tin cup for boiling water."

As he stacked some branches and struck a flint to tinder, Anna began to rummage in her reticule. "Ha!" she exclaimed a moment later, extracting several mashed pieces of gingerbread. "I, too, have been carrying around some forgotten treasures."

A second plunge brought up a handful of honey drops wrapped in brightly colored paper.

His brows rose. "I have always wondered what ladies carry in those things. Aside from vinaigrette, of course."

"A great many useful things, as you can see, replied Anna. "Like. . . a spoon. . . a coil of twine. . . a pair of scissors. . ." She laughed as she added a tiny tin trumpet to the growing pile. "Oh, I had quite forgotten about that."

"Good Lord, what else do you have in there?" Nicholas shook his head in admiration. "A regiment of hussars? We could arm them with shovels instead of sabers and be out of here in a trice."

Turning the reticule upside down, Anna gave it a shake. "No soldiers," she announced, as a last jumble of items spilled from its depth. "Would a bear do?" The wooden toy was painted a whimsical blue, with spots of scarlet for the eyes and nose.

"One of its legs is broken," he pointed out.

"Yes." Anna picked up a bit of engraved silver that had fallen to the ground with the bear. "So is the ring on this watch fob. Still, it is a very pretty design." She hesitated, then reached for his hand and placed both the bear and the fob in his palm. "It's a rather hodgepodge assortment of presents, but it's the spirit that counts. Merry Christmas, Nicholas."

His fingers closed around her offerings. "Thank you," he said softly. The candlelight reflecting off his whiskered jaw seemed to ignite a thousand sparks of fire. "Your gifts, and your spirit, are quite special."

Anna suddenly felt hot all over. "They are just. . . flights of fancy." To hide her burning longing to press her cheek to his, she ducked away and began refilling her reticule. "Surely gentlemen must collect lots of serendipitous things during the course of their travels."

Nicholas cocked his head to one side, setting off another flare of fire. "I never really thought about it. Let us see." Fetching the leather document case from his valise, he emptied it on the blanket. Along with a flutter of papers, out fell a filigree penknife, a small book whose marbled cover had seen better days and a Spanish gold coin.

"This is from a tiny artisan's shop in Lisbon," he mused, fingering the silver blade of the knife. "And the coin—well, after escaping the French patrol, I considered it a lucky charm."

"And the book?" she asked.

"Dante's sonnets. Italian is a lovely language." He opened it and angled the page to the fire. "Here, I shall read one aloud."

The words were like warm honey. Anna closed her eyes, savoring the sweetness of his voice.

"How beautiful," she whispered, when he was done.

A rustle of wool, and suddenly the book was in her lap, along with the knife and the coin.

"Merry Christmas, Anna," said Nicolas softly.

Her lashes flew open. "Oh, I couldn't—"

"The gift of friendship is what Christmas is all about." His fingers twined with hers. "As is sharing. And caring."

"And wishing good will to all men," she added.

He chuckled. "A sentiment you did not hold dear when first we met. With good reason I might add. Though I hope we are now. . . friends."

"I-I have come to think of you as that," said Anna.

Nicholas snuggled her a bit closer. "I have read you poetry, now won't you sing me one of the carols your mother played on this eve?"

Shrew drew in a deep breath. "S-Silent night, holy night. . ." At first the words were hardly more than a zephyr of breath, but they grew stronger as he added a bass note to her clear soprano.

"I should like to hear one in Russian," he encouraged, when they had finished.

"Now it is your turn," she said, once the lilting melody died away.

"Hmmm." He rubbed at his chin. "How about *God Rest Ye Merry Gentlemen* in Dutch?"

When Anna was done giggling at his off-key rendition, she had her own exotic suggestion. "Would you care to hear *Good King Wenceslas* in Polish?"

The winter night was long, but the hours passed quickly as they filled them with songs in a gaggle of other languages. Shared laughter filled the gaps of missing words or melodies. Anna did not quite realize how quickly until Nicholas pulled out his pocket watch and thumbed open its case.

"Good Lord, it is a few minutes past midnight! This calls for a holiday toast." He found the flask of brandy in his bag and passed it to her with a wink. "We must keep the body as well as the spirit warm."

Anna did not need strong drink to feel a delicious heat curl down to her toes. Still, she took a small swallow. And shivered as fire filled her mouth.

Would a kiss from Nicholas taste. . .

Handing it back, she scrabbled to her feet. "Let us go outside for a moment. I-I should like to see if I can spot the Christmas star."

Overhead, the sky was a canopy of black velvet alight with the infinite sparkle of hope. "I wished on a star the night of the storm," she said, as Nicholas came up behind her.

"Make another wish," he murmured.

She bit at her lip. It was cold. "You aren't supposed to say such dreams aloud. Else they won't come true."

He nodded solemnly. "Then how about this—let us both make a wish, and keep it secret."

Silence stretched for several moments. Drawing in a deep breath, Anna spun around and kissed his cheek. "May all your wishes come true, Nicholas," she whispered, then turned and hurried back to the abbey.

But not before slanting a last, longing look at a certain point of light that seemed to twinkle just a bit brighter than all the others.

ANNA AWOKE to early morning sunlight filtering in through the crumbling stone. She smiled as its pale warmth suffused her face, recalling a memorable night.

"Good morning, Nicholas. Now we can truly say Merry Christmas," she called softly.

Hearing no answer, she rubbed the sleep from her eyes and turned to the fire. The coals, rekindled at some point during the night, crackled with a cheery red glow, but the rumpled blanket where he had slept looked stone cold.

Perhaps he had gone to fetch more water, or forage for food...

The sheet of foolscap, stark as snow against her folded cloak, told her otherwise. Her name was scrawled in the same leaden hue that had recently darkened the skies, and she had no doubt the words inside would weigh just as heavily on her heart. She knew, of course, what they would say.

Nicholas was gone.

Drawing the blanket around her shoulders and coaxing the last of the firewood into flames did nothing to ward off the chill seeping into her bones.

Dear Anna, it began. The lettering was smudged and looked to have been written in a hurry. *I am truly sorry that you will awake to find yourself alone on Christmas morning. I should like to have shared one last carol and. . .* He appeared to have crossed out a word or two. *However, having spent most of the night mulling over the situation, it became clear that I must be gone before anyone sees us together. As soon as I reach an inn, I shall see to it that a rescue party is sent. Stick to the following story, and I am confident you will weather any threat to your reputation. Your servants will support whatever account you give, so there is no worry there. . .*

She slowly read over the advice, which detailed how she was to tell everyone, including her uncle, a carefully edited version of the truth.

Say only this, advised Nicholas. *You tried to beat the storm, but the coach suffered a mishap and the storm caught up to you. Your driver went for help, leaving you stranded in the wilds. The snow forced you to take refuge in the abbey ruins, where you decided to wait for the weather to clear and a search party to find you. No one, not the highest stickler or the strictest guardian, will find fault with such actions.*

Anna looked up. Not if she remembered to never, ever make mention of a gentleman companion. Skimming the last few lines, she looked for the ending.

Your friend, N.

A dear friend indeed, she thought, blinking back the pearls of moisture clinging to her lashes. If she had been thinking clearly, she would have realized long before now that the solution he had come up with was the only way to avoid a terrible scandal. But her reason had been clouded by more than a passing snowstorm.

She knew she ought to be very grateful for his unassailable logic and his practical skill at putting a plan into action. And yet a small part of her could not help but regret that he had moved with quite such a show of efficiency. A tiny voice in the back of her head echoed the disappointment, whispering that there had, in fact, been one other alternative to his sudden departure.

But seeing as he had not proposed it, there was no point in dwelling on what might have been. . .

It would only make the future harder to bear.

No, Nicholas was right—it was best that the parting be swift and sure.

Her fingers closed around the small gold coin in her pocket. She would treasure the memory of this Christmas, and the coin's burnished hue would always be a special reminder of a certain blond gentleman. For a glimmering interlude, they had warded off the bleakness of winter with shared friendship.

How could anyone wish for a better gift than that?

Anna smiled through her tears, hoping that he taken away with him something more meaningful than a chipped wooden bear and a broken watch fob. She wanted very much to believe they did not lie discarded by the roadside, along with all thoughts of the time they had spent together.

However, the truth was, she knew so little about his personal life. For all she knew, he had a fiancée waiting to welcome him back to Town.

Or a *chere amie*.

Before her spirits could sink any lower, a shout from the distance recalled her to the present.

"Lady Anna!" Her coachman's familiar voice. True to his word, Nicholas had wasted no time.

"Yes—I am here," she answered. Gathering up her things, she stood and began to stamp out the last flickering of the fire.

NICHOLAS SENT the coachman to fetch the horses, so he would have a chance to speak to Anna alone. As he slipped through the entrance to the abbey, he noted that the letter was still in her hand.

"There's been a slight change in plans—I hope you don't mind." He could feel that his smile was slightly lopsided. So were his nerves. The beating of his heart had knocked them all to flinders. "I found I could not bear the idea of leaving you alone on Christmas." His feet shuffled in the snow. "Or on any day, for that matter. That is to say, the idea of a future with you. . . and me. . . together. . ."

He cleared his throat. "Dash it all, for a diplomat supposedly skilled in the nuances of language, I am making a real hash of this."

Anna let out her breath. "I think you are doing just fine." She smiled "Please go on."

Encouraged, he pulled her into his arms. "Then I shall stop beating around the bush. I love you, Anna. More dearly than words can ever express." He feathered a gossamer kiss to her brow, her cheek, and then possessed her moth in a far more through one.

It was several minutes before he spoke again. "Will you marry me, sweeting? You have hinted that your guardian has other plans for you. And as a matter of fact, my father wishes for me to— well, never mind. It doesn't matter now." His arms tightened around her. "To the Devil with the expectations of others. We have been given a great gift in finding each other, one too precious to let be taken from our grasp."

Tears, like ice jewels, sparkled on her cheek. "I love you, Nicholas. I wish with all my heart to be your wife." Her chin took on the defiant little tilt he had come to adore. "And if my guardian seeks to make an international incident—"

"Leave the negotiations to me, my dear, said Nicholas firmly. "I will take care that our two countries do not come to blows."

CHAPTER 6

"*You* are late."

"Yes, well, I ran into a spot of difficulty." Biting back a more acid comment to his father, Nicholas settled for a retort that was only mildly sarcastic. "Next time you wish to summon me during the depths of December, kindly negotiate a truce with the weather gods so they don't interfere with your plans."

"Hmmph." Without looking up, the Earl of Royster opened another portfolio and fanned the contents across his blotter. "Was that, perchance, meant as a criticism?"

"With all due respect, sir. . ."

His father shuffled a sheaf of documents into order.

"Yes," replied Nicholas loudly. "It bloody well was."

The earl put down his pen. And let out a chuckle. "That was not the most diplomatic of replies."

"I was not speaking as a diplomat." Nicholas did, however, moderate his tone to something less than a shout. "Sir."

Leaning back in his chair, Royster quirked a silvery brow and fixed his son with The Stare. It was a look the earl had perfected over the years, using it with ruthless regularity to reduce friend and foe alike to quaking in their boots.

Unmoved for once, Nicholas simply stared back.

"Well, well, well. It appears you have a bit of fire in your belly after all." Steepling his fingers, the earl tapped them against his chin. "I was beginning to wonder whether there was any sort of spark there, or merely a lump of ice."

"I was under the impression that you considered cold reason to be the cornerstone of duty and diplomacy."

"So I do." The corners of his father's mouth twitched ever so slightly. "But that is not to say one must always be a Stoic. There is nothing wrong with showing a bit of passion from time to time."

"I am very glad to hear you say so sir." Like his Christmas journey, the conversation was taking all sorts of unexpected twists and turns, but Nicholas refused to be sidetracked. "For that surely means you can have no objection to my telling you I've decided not to pay court to some stranger."

The humor disappeared from Royster's face. "Now, now, there is no reason to be hasty."

"I've had a rather prolonged interlude in which to give your request careful thought," replied Nicholas. "And the answer is, I won't do it."

"If we discuss this in a calm and rational manner," replied his father. "I'm sure we can come to an acceptable compromise."

"You may as well save your breath, Father. I can't imagine any argument that could change my mind." Nicholas angled his gaze to the portrait over the mantel. Lud, did all Wrenfax men look so imperious? "You see, I have made other plans."

The earl's brows angled higher and The Stare took on a more pronounced squint. "The count will be deeply disappointed if I tell him you won't attend the ball he's giving in the young lady's honor. Indeed, he might take it as an insult, not only to his family, but to Mother Russia."

"Russia?" Nicholas jerked his head around.

"A very large chunk of frozen tundra to our east, populated with bears, beards and boyars," came the dry reply. "Need I remind you that the alliance is of strategic importance to our country?"

"No, I am fully aware of how much is at stake. But the truth is—'

He was saved from having to explain himself by a muffled roar from just outside the library.

"Step aside, lest you wish your spindly shanks to be fed to the wolves! I tell you, the earl will see me, regardless of the hour."

The family butler, who did have rather reedy legs, had a hunted look on his face as he opened the door a crack. "Milord, I tried to tell the, er, gentleman, that you could not be interrupted, but he wouldn't take no for an answer."

"*Nyet* indeed!" thundered the intruder.

"It is quite alright, Belmont, your limbs are safe from snapping jaws for the time being," said Royster. "You may allow the count to come in."

The butler pressed his frail shoulders against the paneled oak to avoid being flattened by the onrushing figure.

With his greatcoat skirling around his high-top boots and the capes flapping like raucous ravens around his broad shoulders the count appeared even larger than he really was.

"Merry Christmas, Yevgeny," called the earl "Won't you join me and my son in a toast to good cheer and—"

"Nyet!" roared the count. "I cannot be merry at a time like this! I am—how you say—dis. . ."

"Distraught?" suggested Nicholas. His own nerves were none too steady at the moment.

"Yes! Distraught! Otherwise I would not descend upon your home and your holiday like a ravening bear. Of all my English acquaintances, you are the man I have confidence in, Royster."

"I will help in any way I can. What is the trouble?"

"My niece was due to arrive in London the day before yesterday, but she has gone missing!"

The earl's expression sobered considerably. Setting aside the decanter of brandy, he sought to allay his visitor's agitation. "I am sure there is no real cause for alarm. I know for a fact that the bad weather has delayed a number of travelers."

"Father," said Nicolas.

Neither man paid any heed to Nicholas's quiet murmur.

The count's composure took a sharp turn for the worse as he started to pace before the fire. "One of the men I sent out in search of her discovered her coach, abandoned on a stretch of desolate road."

"We—" began the earl.

"We were just coming to tell you that all is well and that your niece is quite safe." Nicholas fixed the earl with a steady gaze and waggled a brow. "Weren't we, Father?"

The Stare took on a peculiar tilt, but years of diplomatic experience allowed the earl to reply without missing a beat. "Indeed. We were. But seeing as Nicholas deserves all the credit, I will defer to him in explaining all the details." Folding his hands upon his blotter, Royster added dryly, "I confess, Yevgeny, I am as anxious as you are to hear exactly how he managed the feat."

Count Federov, who had been rendered momentarily speechless, recovered enough to sputter, "You mean to say my Anna is with you?"

"At the moment, sir, she is downstairs with our housekeeper, freshening up from her ordeal."

An odd rumble started deep in the count's throat, and his hands began to twitch.

It was, decided Nicholas, a reaction that did not bode well for peace and harmony. In one fell swoop both his limbs and any prospect of a treaty between England and Russia looked about to be ripped asunder.

"Grrrr. . ." With two quick strides, the count crossed the carpet. "Thank God! I am eternally grateful to you, *tovarich*."

Nicholas found himself enveloped in a bear hug and lifted off his feet.

"Royster," called Count Federov, his craggy face

wreathed in a joyous smile. "You told me that your son was a remarkable young man, but you were too modest by half. Ha! I do not know how he discovered my plight, but to have acted so quickly and decisively." He shook his head. "It's a miracle.

"Sometimes even I am astounded by my son's resourcefulness," drawled the earl. "Er, perhaps if you would allow him a breath of air, we may hear all about the dramatic rescue. It promises to be a fascinating tale."

"Yes! Of course."

Nicholas hit the floor with a thump. His knees wobbled, but he kept his balance and cleared his throat. He did not need to look at the earl to know that he was treading a very fine line. One small misstep and he would go from being a hero to a goat.

A goat staked out on the Siberian steppes for the wolves to devour.

"It was a dark and stormy night, Count Federov…"

The earl gave a small cough. "Forgive me—something must have lodged in my throat."

A laugh, unless Nicholas was much mistaken. His reproachful glance was met with a nod of contrition.

"Do go on," murmured Royster, after swallowing a sip of his brandy.

"Through the swirl of the snow I happened to spot a wink of light…" His secret delight in the novels of Mrs. Radcliffe and the Minerva Press was now proving quite useful in cobbling together a suspenseful narrative. "Then, above the howl of the snowstorm, I heard a faint cry for help…"

Jaw slightly agape, Federov perched his bulk on the edge of the desk and leaned forward.

"Half frozen, and on death's door from the blow he had suffered trying to stave off the falling tree, the coachman lay unconscious inside the coach," went Nicholas. "The stalwart young lady had braved the elements to save him from a certain demise, but with the weather worsening, things were looking very grim." For the most part, Nicholas was able to adhere to the spirit, if not the letter, of the truth, with just a few omissions and embellishments to gloss over the unconventional parts.

His father's brows crept fractionally higher as the tale went on, but he remained silent. The count was a good deal more voluble, interrupting every few moments with a gasp or a mutter in his native tongue.

"Extraordinary!" he exclaimed, when Nicholas was done recounting the arrival in Grosvenor Square.

"Extraordinary," echoed the earl.

"With such admirable talents, I think your son is destined for a brilliant career in your foreign service, Royster," said the count.

"Yes, well, I have always stressed to him that one of the keys to success in diplomacy is creativity—along with the ability to think on one's feet."

"Actually, I'm not quite finished," said Nicholas.

Federov looked slightly perplexed. "There is more?"

"I have left until last mentioning that I have asked Anna for her hand in marriage."

He was rather amused by the stunned silence that

followed the announcement. It wasn't often that two such gentlemen could be rendered speechless.

"And she has accepted?" asked Fedorov warily.

"Yes, sir."

"Without —how do you say—fireworks? Or your having to call in a regiment of the Preobrazhensky Guards?"

"As you know, sir, the use of force is always the last resort for a diplomat," replied Nicholas, a twinkle lighting his eye as he clasped his hands behind his back. "I was able to persuade your niece to say 'yes' through the means of rational discourse."

The count made a wry face. "Perhaps you have rescued the wrong young lady." An instant later the grimace was gone, replaced by a grin. "I think I shall accept that drink after all, Royster. It seems we have much to celebrate on this most joyous of your holidays."

Turning to Nicholas, he inclined a low bow. "It may not yet be Christmas in my country, but you have given me a most wondrous gift, Lord Killingworth. I believe Anna shall be very happy with you. And for that I thank you with all my heart."

"Rather it is I who should be thanking you, sir." Nicholas turned to the earl. "And you, Father. I consider myself blessed with miraculous good fortune. Who would have dreamed that in the midst of darkness and storm I would come upon the light of my life?"

He raised his glass, savoring the blazing fire and beaming smiles through the warm glow of the brandy. "To family. Both present and future."

The clink of crystal had not yet subsided when Fedorov proposed another round of toasts. "It seems that tomorrow's ball will take on an extra note of good cheer as we will be able to announce a pair of alliances between our two countries."

He winked at the earl. "After much discussion, my delegation agreed to your latest proposal and the papers were signed this morning."

Nicholas stifled a laugh. "I trust they plan to award each of you a medal for your consummate skill at handling delicate negotiations."

His father maintained a straight face, save for a tiny waggle of his brow. "Oh, I believe Yevgeny and I have reward enough."

It was not snow but a blur of bright silks and satins, that swirled through the ballroom, and the brilliant sparkling of light came from a myriad of crystal chandeliers rather than ice.

"It is like a scene from a fairy tale," whispered Anna as Nicholas spun her through another series of twirls.

"Our journey most certainly had a storybook ending, my love," he replied, his eyes dancing with a depth of emotion that made her heart skip a beat.

"Complete with a dashing hero who sweeps the lady off her feet," she whispered.

How had she ever viewed him as just another pompous prig? Now she saw only his kindness, his strength, his humor. His chiseled features, softened by the curl of golden locks and a devilish smile, were not bad to look at either. "You had a few small details of your story wrong. Your father is not such an ogre after all."

The Earl of Royster, resplendent in ivory silk waistcoat embroidered with a forest of fir trees, appeared not at all perturbed to be holding a glass of champagne instead of a sheaf of government papers. "He dances quite beautifully and told me several very amusing stories about you and your first pony."

Nicholas gave a mock wince. "Yet another instance of me falling smack on my rump."

"As for your mother. . . " Anna touched the pale peach flower pinned to his lapel, then glanced at the countess, who was dancing with Count Federov. "To think she spent the summer and fall creating a new species of roses specially for you. And it was very ingenious of her to design a portable greenhouse so that several of the bushes could be transported from Yorkshire."

"Yes, I have learned much these past few days, not only about myself, but about those around me. We all have facets we have grown used to keeping under wraps. Sometimes what we need is a challenge to bring them to light."

"And sometimes what we need is a miracle from above." Anna could not help but think back on her own doubts and fears. "When I saw that first star in the heavens, I wished for a guardian angel instead of a guardian uncle. What I got was an even greater blessing—I got you."

"We have both been blessed," he murmured. "I trust that we shall look out for each other. I hope I shall always be a guardian of your happiness, my love, and you of mine. But

I do not mean for this to be a one-sided match. You have my solemn promise that your opinions and wishes shall always be as important as mine."

He grinned. "After all, my experience in the art of diplomacy has shown me that the prospect for harmony is always best when both parties have an equal say in things."

"Be careful what you wish for," teased Anna.

"Truly, I have nothing more to ask for."

The curl of his lips sent a sizzle of heat right down to the toes of her dancing slippers.

"I've been given the most precious gifts of all. Love, hope, happiness. Christmas is truly a time of miracles." His smile turned a touch more tentative. "I know that for you it has been a time of sorrow, but—"

Anna pressed the palm of her glove to his cheek. "I think I have come to understand another message of the season. Loss is part of life, but we must never allow its darkness to extinguish the light in our hearts. From now on, Christmas will always be a season of great joy, as long as we share it together."

He suddenly spun to a stop in the middle of the ballroom and swept her up in his arms.

"Nicholas! People are staring!"

"Sometimes it doesn't hurt to bend the rules, remember?" he murmured, cutting off her laughing protest with a long and lingering kiss.

Anna arched into his arms. When at last his lips released hers, he murmured, "Speaking of protocol, would you be opposed to having our nuptials on Christmas?

"Christmas?" Her face fell. "Y-you wish to wait a whole year to be married?"

His eyes lit with unholy amusement. "Indeed not. I was thinking of the *Russian* Christmas. Which is less than two weeks away. I have procured a special license, and your uncle has assured me he has no objection."

"Considering that ours has been a very unorthodox courtship, it seems a very fitting day for a celebration," she answered.

"What a lucky family we shall be having Christmas come twice a year!"

"Every day will feel like Christmas with you by my side, my dear Nicholas," said Anna.

"Amen to that," answered Nicholas.

And then he kissed her again.

A GATHERING OF GIFTS

CHAPTER 1

"Oh, show a little spirit, Charles! Must you always be a cautious as a church mouse creeping past a sleeping tabby?" Without waiting for a reply, the young lady slapped her crop against her horse's flank and sent the high-strung stallion hurtling toward the towering stonewall.

"The trouble is not *my* lack of spirit, but rather *your* overabundance of it," muttered her companion as he spurred his own horse forward. "Ye God, I fear that if you don't learn to rein in some of your less laudable tendencies, my dear Emma, it's going to land you in the suds—and sooner than later."

His jaw unclenched slightly on seeing that she had cleared the obstacle without mishap, but the slip and clatter of hooves on the slippery ground quickly brought a fresh grimace to his face. The fact that a patch of ice nearly threw his stallion off stride as they approached the tumble of stones did nothing to improve his temper.

It took a firm hand to ensure that neither of them came to grief because of the treacherous footing, and by the time he pulled to a halt beside his cousin, Charles, Viscount Lawrance felt his patience about to snap.

"You see, there was nothing to worry about!" Lady Emma Pierson gave a toss of her blonde curls, causing the jaunty little feather adorning her riding cap to brush against the shoulder of her stylish-frogged jacket. She grinned at her cousin. "Ajax and Orion have jumped far higher fences on countless occasions. Come, there's a path up ahead with several more obstacles and a stretch where we can race—"

"Nothing to worry about?" repeated Charles angrily, as he drew to a halt beside her. "The deuce take it, Emma, it was a foolish risk! You had no idea what lay beyond the stones. Why, if the ground had been a trifle more icy, both Ajax and you might have broken your necks." His mouth thinned. "You may have little regard for your own well-being," he went on in a low growl, "but such a splendid animal deserves more consideration."

At the first volley of sharp words, the smile disappeared from Emma's face. "You needn't lecture me as if you were one of my former governesses. I don't need *anyone* to tell me how to go on—especially you, Charles, who are only two years my senior."

She drew in a sharp breath. "I'm not a child anymore. In case you have forgotten, I have already had a Season in Town. A very successful one, at that," she added with a decided sniff.

"Then, show you have gained some sense as well as years, Em. You're right—you are no longer fourteen and dragging the rest of us into one bumblebroth after another with your impetuous actions. It's time to stop acting like a headstrong little hellion, with no mind for aught but your own whims."

Her eyes narrowed, a flash of emotion sparking beneath her lashes. "The rest of the gentlemen of the ton don't seem to find such fault with my behavior," she retorted.

"Don't be so sure," he shot back. "As a matter of fact, I had been meaning to broach the subject at some point during my visit, so it may as well be now." There was a brief pause. "An undesirable reputation, once garnered, is not nearly so easy to shed as a gown whose color no longer pleases you."

Beneath the wind-whipped color, Emma's cheeks went very pale. "H-How can you imply such a horrid thing! I—I had more admirers dancing attendance on me than any of the other young ladies making their come-out."

"Oh, there's no denying that your beauty—not to speak of your lineage and dowry—attracts gentlemen like honey draws a swarm of bees," replied her cousin, the edge of anger replaced by a note of concern. "People may fawn over your looks and your fortune, but around the clubs, there are whispers that your behavior is becoming a tad less admirable."

Emma blinked.

"I may as well be blunt," he continued. "Since your mother's death, your father has indulged in your every whim, and it has done more harm than good. To be brutally honest, you are in danger of becoming a spoiled brat, Emma. I say such a thing because I know that, at heart, you are no such thing." Charles sighed. "But of late, your actions do you no credit."

Her lips quivered slightly. "I—I don't know what you mean."

"Don't you?" he asked quietly.

She turned in profile, the brim of her hat shadowing her face.

"Let me remind you of just a few incidents from the past Season. Demanding that poor Palmerston let you drive his team of grays along Rotten Row nearly resulted in Lady Haverstock being seriously injured."

"She. . . she should have moved out of the way a bit quicker," responded Emma.

"Lud, the poor lady is nearly eighty!" He smoothed at the collar of his coat, though the crease remained on his brow. "Then, there was the poem you composed about Miss Taverhill and recited at Lady Jermaine's gala ball. That was truly not well-done of you."

"But she *does* look like a Maypole, especially when she is dressed in cherry and white stripes!" Despite the quickness of her retort, Emma did not quite bring her gaze to meet his. "It was all in good fun. Everyone laughed."

"Everyone except Miss Taverhill," Charles said quietly. "I happened to see her sobbing in a corner of the deserted library, and her brother mentioned that it was nigh on a sennight before she had the courage to appear in public again."

His lips compressed in a tight line. "If you had stopped to think, you would have realized it was a cruel thing to do."

"It was just a jest," she replied stiffly. "I meant no harm."

"Perhaps not. But you caused hurt and humiliation to someone who deserved neither. What I'm trying to say is that your behavior is becoming increasingly self-absorbed. Which is a pity, because the Emma I know and love is not that sort of person. I would hate to think that superficial flatteries could seduce you from being true to yourself."

Emma turned back to face him, and for an instant he saw a flash of emotion flicker beneath her lashes—though it was gone too quickly for him to read.

"Christmas is supposed to be a time of good cheer and jolly fun," she said in a brittle voice. "If you find my company unpleasant, perhaps you would rather be elsewhere than Telford Manor for the holidays."

A sigh escaped his lips. "You know that I find you no such thing, Emma. If I didn't like you so well, I wouldn't bother speaking of my concerns. Trust me, I take no pleasure from bringing them up."

Her hand tightened on the butt of her crop. "Is that all? Or have you any other criticisms to bring up?"

"No. I've said my piece and am done with it. However, I hope you will think on it." He forced a smile. "Now, let us ride on before the horses take a chill."

He gathered his reins and quickly sought to point the conversation in a new direction as well. "Your father mentioned that there is finally someone in residence at Hawthorne House. Have you met the family?"

Emma shook her head as they moved off. "No, but I understand that the gentleman is some junior officer who only recently sold out when he inherited the baron's title." She shrugged. "Heddy Tillson says he's brought his widowed sister and her child to stay with him, and by the glimpse she caught of them in the village, they don't look to have much polish or blunt. It is too bad—we could have done with some lively company in the area, but it sounds as if they will prove to be dull as dishwater."

Her cousin bit back a reproach about rushing to judgment, especially when it was based on the observations of such a flighty pea-goose as Heddy Tillson.

"Perhaps you will be surprised," he murmured.

Ignoring the remark, Emma urged her mount into a brisk trot. "If we go left here," she called over her shoulder, gesturing toward the fork in the trail, "we shall drop down into the orchards by Hawthorne House. The recent storm has left several fallen trees that make for a bracing ride."

"Let us go right, then, and continue on to the open fields," he replied. "The ground is too frozen to chance any more jumping—"

But Emma had already spurred her horse forward. Her crop flashed through the air, and Ajax thundered off at a dead gallop.

Charles already knew which turn Emma would choose before the stallion was halfway there. For a moment he was sorely tempted to turn back to the manor house and leave her to face any consequences that might befall her. However, gentlemanly scruples won out over pique. The weather looked to be turning even worse, so after letting fly with a few choice epithets, he followed after her, though at a more circumspect pace.

The worst of his anger had been vented along with the curses. It was hard to stay mad at Emma for long, for despite her faults, he considered her the best of friends—smart, funny, loyal, and good-natured, regardless of the criticisms he had voiced earlier.

If only she would. . .

Even from a distance, the cry of pain was sharply audible. But by the time Charles had reached the spot where the riderless stallion sidled in nervous agitation, and had vaulted down from his saddle, there was not a sound coming from his cousin's prostrate form.

"My God, Emma! Can you hear me?" he demanded as he knelt down beside her.

Her eyes slowly fluttered open. "Y-yes." She bit her lip and struggled to sit up. "I think it's just a bit of bruising—to both my rump and my pride. But is Ajax unharmed? I shall never forgive myself if—"

"Yes, yes, he's fine." Charles slipped his arm under her shoulders, but prevented her from rising. "Don't move for a moment. You've had a nasty spill." The breath he had been holding came out in a rush of relief. "Lord, another few inches and you might have been killed," he added in a low voice, eyeing the jagged stumps of broken branches poking up from the fallen oak.

"You may go ahead and say that I would have thoroughly deserved such a fate," she said with a tremor in her voice. "I-I. . ."

"Silly poppet." He cut off her words by burying her face

in the folds of his jacket. Her fashionable little military style shako had been dislodged by the fall, and his fingers began to gently stroke her tangled curls. "Life should be sadly flat without my favorite cousin to brangle with."

Emma stifled a sob. "I know that I've been. . ."

"Shhhh," he soothed. "We shall discuss that some other time. Right now, do you think you can manage to stand?"

"I think so, if you will give me a hand." With a game smile, she attempted to get to her feet, but as soon as her right foot touched the ground, she bit back a scream of agony and collapsed against his chest, her face ashen with pain.

"I-I fear it is worse than I thought," she gasped.

Charles helped her lie back down on the frozen earth. "Hawthorne House is not far away. I shall have to ride there to fetch help and to send word for a doctor. Will you be all right for a bit?"

She nodded.

He peeled off his riding coat and tucked it over her chest. "That's the spirit. I knew I could depend on you not to fall into a fit of vapors," he replied with a wan grin. "I'll be back as soon as I can."

Emma shifted slightly on the hard ground, and an unladylike word escaped her lips. Several, in fact. She winced, thinking that if Charles had overheard such language, he would no doubt ring down another peal upon her head.

Not that it was possible to sink any lower in his esteem.

The uncomfortable thought caused her to move once more, sending a stab of pain through her right ankle. What hurt more, however, was the memory of her cousin's frank words.

Was he right? she wondered, blinking back a tear. Had she really turned into the selfish monster he described?

A part of her longed to shrug off such criticism. Perhaps he was merely upset because she had not spent as much time with him during the whirlwind months in London as in the past. After all, she had been one of the leading belles of the beau monde's Season. Countless gentlemen had vied for the honor of leading her out on the dance floor. They had laughed at her bon mots, applauded her performances on the pianoforte, and complimented her on her riding skills...

Praise heaped on praise—according to everyone around her, she could do no wrong.

Surely Charles *must* be mistaken, she assured herself.

Such a conclusion made her feel infinitely better, and so she chose to ignore the tiny voice in the back of her head, which whispered that Charles was never petty or mean-spirited. Instead, as she drifted into unconsciousness, she heard only the echo of all the honeyed flattery and sugared praise that had come her way.

Such sweet reveries were rudely interrupted by a rough shake of her shoulders.

"Come, now. Open your eyes!"

Emma groggily did as ordered—and wasn't so sure the decision had been a wise one.

It was not Charles whose face loomed only inches from hers, but rather that of a perfect stranger.

Actually, he was not perfect at all, she decided, once her eyes were able to focus. His face was lean and angular, its color unfashionably bronzed by the sun. A shock of unruly black hair fell over his brow, accentuating the sharp, aquiline line of his nose. His chiseled lips looked to be full and well formed, but it was difficult to be sure, as they were presently pursed in a grim scowl.

No less grim was the piercing gaze he had fixed upon her face. She squirmed slightly under the severe scrutiny, though it was impossible to break away from the glittering intensity of his hazel eyes.

No, she realized, they were not exactly hazel, for they had the most interesting flecks of molten gold—

"Well, she appears to be conscious." The stranger looked away, and Emma was vaguely aware of Charles hovering somewhere behind him. His gaze quickly shifted back to her and then to the massive tree trunk and the patch of ice in front of it.

"Good Lord," he muttered with ill-concealed disdain. "How could anyone be so cork-brained as to attempt such a stunt in these conditions?"

She managed to prop herself up on one elbow. "I'll have you know, sir, that I am accorded to be an *excellent* rider."

The stranger's brow arched up. "It would appear that such praise is completely unwarranted." There was a slight pause. "Thank God your horse wasn't seriously injured."

Emma gasped, first at the rudeness of his words, and then at the fact that he started to run his hands down the

length of her arms and then her legs. "How dare you—
ouch!"

The stranger leaned back on his haunches. "I don't think any bones are broken," he said to Charles. "But the ankle appears to be badly sprained. I suppose we shall have to move her to Hawthorne House for the present. Fetch her horse while I take her up."

"But—" began Emma. The protest was muffled in the folds of his coat as he lifted her into his arms with one easy motion. To her dismay, she saw that her cousin had jumped to obey the man's curt command.

"Put me down!" she snapped. "I do not wish for you to—"

"Stop squirming," he ordered. "Lest you wish to add to your collection of bruises by taking a second tumble to the ground." His arms drew her closer to his chest. "Though perhaps another thump would knock some sense into that brainbox of yours."

She fell silent and ceased her struggling, taking care to avoid any further eye contact with the stranger. Harder to ignore was the corded strength of his shoulders or the heat emanating from his broad chest. From her precarious position, it was clear that he was at least several inches taller than her cousin and a good deal more muscular. Despite her own considerable height, he carried her through the orchard as if she weighed no more than a feather.

"Odious man," she whispered under her breath, thinking of his last rude comment. For an instant, Emma thought she detected a faint chuckle, but when she ventured a surreptitious peek at his face, the same hard expression was etched on his features.

Leaning back, she closed her eyes. Awful though he was, the ordeal would be over in a trice, she reminded herself. Thank heavens one of her father's carriages would soon be arriving to take her home.

*N*oel Trumbull, newly acceded to the title of Lord Kirtland, stared out the mullioned windows and let out a harried sigh. Of all the dratted luck! He had enough to worry about without being stuck dancing attendance on some spoiled heiress, no matter that she had hair like spun gold and eyes as blue as the Mediterranean Sea in summer.

His lips compressed. Oh, yes, Lady Emma Pierson was attractive all right. And the wealthy heiress damn well knew it, be reminded himself. Even though he had only spent a week in London on his return from the Peninsula, he had heard Lady Emma's name mentioned as being one of the brightest Diamonds of the Season. And then he had seen her from afar at Lady Hightower's ball—and had felt the air squeezed from his lungs.

She was, in a word, breathtaking. The perfect picture of loveliness, grace, and vitality.

What a pity that her beauty appeared to be only skin-deep.

Granted, he had been inclined to think ill of her before ever meeting her, as his good friend Augustus Taverhill had mentioned how Lady Emma had written a hurtful poem about his sister.

One mistake could, of course, be forgiven as an error of judgment. But his first impression confirmed that she was both arrogant and waspish—traits he abhorred in anyone, be they male or female. He could only hope that one of her father's carriages would soon be arriving to take her home.

"Lord Kirtland. . ."

Noel quickly turned and crossed the carpet. But such hopes were quickly dashed by the terse pronouncement of the doctor examining Lady Emma, who was now lying on the sofa of his drawing room.

"Tis a nasty twist, Lady Emma," he announced with a cluck of his tongue. "I'm afraid there is no question of you being moved until the swelling has gone down."

But—" began both Emma and Noel at once.

They stopped short. Noel then clamped his jaw firmly shut, regretting that surprise had wrested any show of emotion out of him. He moved to the hearth, determined to keep to himself just how unwelcome the announcement was.

The last thing he needed was yet another responsibility weighing on his shoulders as Christmas approached. It would be difficult enough creating the proper spirit of the holidays without the presence of a conceited stranger in their home.

It quickly became clear that the young lady was no more pleased with the announcement than he was.

"I would not dream of imposing on this gentleman's gracious hospitality any longer than I already have," she said with unveiled sarcasm. "Surely my ankle can tolerate a short carriage ride."

The doctor shook his head. "Absolutely not." He pushed his spectacles back up to the bridge of his nose. "The injury should heal without any lasting ill effects, but only if great care is taken now. And even if I were to consider the request, it would not be possible, given the state of the lane leading here. It has been unused for so long that it is hardly better than a cart track. Any ride over such jolts and ruts could cause further damage."

"Charles could take me up on Orion—" she began.

The doctor waved away the suggestion. "Now, don't be foolish, Lady Emma. You are very fortunate that Hawthorne House has lately become inhabited. You will be quite comfortable here."

"Ha!" she muttered under her breath.

"It will only be for a short time," piped up Charles, slanting an uneasy glance at Noel. "That is, if you have no objections, Lord Kirtland."

"It appears there is little choice in the matter," he replied grimly. With a tone designed to match the young lady's earlier mocking politeness, he added, "Though I must warn Lady Emma that we are hardly able to entertain her in the style to which she is no doubt accustomed."

He watched Emma's lovely features twist into a scowl. "But it's not fair!" she exclaimed. "Robert and his friends are arriving soon for the holidays. And Papa. And your friend Mr. Harkness. Just think of all the fun I shall be missing." Her lower lip began to quiver. "And my ankle is beginning to throb unmercifully."

Noel couldn't help himself. "Dear me, life is indeed horribly fair, to have heaped such unconscionable suffering upon your poor head," he muttered under his breath.

"I shall ride back this afternoon with a number of your things, Em," said Charles quickly, seeking to forestall any further comment from his cousin. "And, of course, we shall all come visit and spend as much time—"

"No. I'm afraid that will not be possible." Noel folded his arms across his chest and calmly regarded the two startled faces that turned his way. "My sister is still recovering from the death of her husband. I'll not have my family and household turned on its ear because the Duke of Telford's daughter imagines she cannot live without constant amusement. One visitor, for one hour a day. That is all I will allow."

His eyes met hers. "You'll survive."

Emma's chin came up. "Shall you keep me on bread-and-water rations, too? I imagine that is all a man of your strict temperament would deign to feed his troops."

Noel gave a humorless laugh. "If bread and water was to be had, my troops were infinitely grateful for it, Lady Emma. On the battlefields of the Peninsula, liveried servants do not appear at the ring of a bell with silver salvers."

Noting she at least had the grace to color, he went on, "Neither will they here. Now, if you will excuse me, I have some rather more important matters to attend to."

Turning on his heel, he quit the room, making no attempt to prevent the door from closing with a pronounced thump.

That should make it clear to the pampered little minx that he would not dance attendance on her like everyone else did, he thought as he walked down the narrow corridor toward the kitchen. It was quite evident that "no" was not a word with which she was intimately acquainted.

But she did have some spirit, he was forced to admit. He had half expected her to turn into a watering pot or lapse into a fit of hysterics on hearing his announcement. Instead, she had met his deliberate roughness with a show of spunk.

A faint smile crept to his lips. Her comment about bread and water showed she had a sharp sense of humor as well. And more than a little courage. Although he had made light of her injury, he knew it must be a very painful one. In all fairness to her, she had born the discomfort with a soldier's fortitude, making no complaint until that moment.

He made a wry face. Perhaps the young lady had more to her than he had first thought. However, that was hardly any concern to him. As he had told Lady Emma and her cousin, he had a good deal of other things to occupy his mind.

Picking up the hammer and chisel that he had left lying

on the scarred pine table, he turned his attention back to trying to loosen a rusted bolt on the door of the iron stove. The house had been sadly neglected by his predecessors, but until he could make a final assessment of the late baron's finances, he was determined not to incur expenses that he could ill afford. For the time being, most of the rambling structure would remain closed off, save for the small wing where he and his family had taken up residence.

It, too, needed a good deal of attention to make it a snug place to live, so he had determined to do much of the menial labor himself. He didn't mind—he disliked being idle, and the work would keep him busy until he could make long range plans and see about hiring a proper crew of workmen. Besides, it gave him a sense of satisfaction to see the improvements take shape with each passing day.

By Christmas Eve, he vowed, the fires would burn without smoking, the draperies would be free of dust, and the hearths would be polished and hung with greenery. He wanted Anna and Toby to have a snug, cheery home in which to celebrate their first holiday without James.

But try as he might to concentrate on the task at hand, he couldn't keep his thoughts from drifting back to their unexpected guest.

She was no milk-and-water miss, that was for sure. He preferred a lady who had opinions of her own, but whether Lady Emma's spirit was indicative of merely a headstrong nature or other, more exemplary qualities, he wasn't sure.

What he did know was that it was hard to find fault with the lush fullness of her lips, even when they were pursed in a pout. As for the spark in her eyes , it was intriguing.

To his dismay, he found it impossible to banish the picture of a mass of spun-gold curls and the way her chin came up in a saucy tilt when she was angry. He supposed it was only natural to feel the stirrings of physical attraction for a beautiful lady, but his reaction to this particular one only caused his mood to turn blacker.

It grew even worse when a careless swing of the hammer caught a sharp blow to his thumb. Swearing under his breath, Noel gave it a shake, then clenched his jaw. No doubt Lady Emma already had a legion of besotted young men making cakes of themselves over her.

He would not add to their ranks.

And yet, whatever the young lady's faults, she radiated a certain vitality. Lord, if only a single spark of Lady Emma's lively fire might be rekindled in Anne .

The kitchen door opened, and his sister and her young son came in with a basket full of fresh-cut pine boughs.

"Joseph says there has been some kind of accident," she said in concern as she fumbled with the knots of her bonnet.

Noel pulled a face. "It's nothing serious. Telford's daughter has taken a tumble from her horse and twisted an ankle. The doctor and her cousin are with her now."

He stood up and ran his hand through his hair. "The bad news is that it appears we are to be saddled with the lady until she is well enough to be moved."

"Oh, dear, I had best go see if there is anything I can do to be of help."

"Anne!"

His sharp tone caused her to stop in mid-stride.

"The chit is not at death's door. Much as she might wish it, she's not in need of someone to wait hand and foot on her."

"But I don't mind—"

"That's not the point," he continued doggedly. "You are as much a guest under my roof as she is. It's bad enough that you must help with household tasks until I see what staff we can afford, but I won't have you reduced to serving as a maid for some pampered aristocrat."

Anne's brow furrowed. "Surely the young lady cannot be as bad as all that."

"Ha," he muttered, then added another expression for good measure.

His young nephew had been listening to the exchange with great interest.

"The Devil take it?" he repeated. "What is he taking, Uncle Noel? And where is he taking it?"

"Tobias!" chided his mother. "You are not to use such improper language."

"Sorry," growled Noel with an apologetic shrug. "I shall try to set a better example." Reaching out, he ruffled the lad's tousled curls. "The Devil is taking me to task for using such horrid cant in front of your mother. Let it be a lesson of what you should *not* say in the presence of a lady."

His nephew gave a solemn nod.

"Now, I need another man to give me a hand in fixing the stove. Will you help hold my tools while I work at this bolt?"

Toby gave a delighted grin and turned away to take up the hammer.

"I could not wish for a better example for my son, Noel," said Anne quietly, a wistful smile stealing across her pale features. "Save of course for. . ." Her voice broke off, and she looked away.

"Well," she continued after a moment in a brisker voice. "While you two are occupied here, I best see about setting one of the extra bedchambers in readiness for our guest."

"I vow, Charles, I would rather hop back to Telford Manor on one leg than stay here," grumbled Emma as the doctor left the small drawing room. She looked at her cousin through lowered lashes and gave a long sigh. "Orion's gait is smooth as silk. Surely you could take me up behind you without any trouble."

"Oh, no, you don't." He crossed his arms. "You may wrap half the young bucks in Town around your little finger, but I know you too well to succumb to your wiles, Em. One disaster is enough for the day."

He paused for a fraction as she fixed him with an imploring look. "You heard the doctor. It would be foolish to risk further damage, so I'll not be swayed by any pleading or wheedling. The baron is right—several days of quiet recuperation here will not be an undue hardship."

"But he is an odious man!"

"Because he stands firm in the face of your entreaties?" Charles countered with a glimmer of a smile. "Unlike any other gentlemen of your acquaintance."

"Wretch," she muttered. "So you truly mean to abandon me here with an ill-tempered martinet and a grieving widow?"

He didn't budge.

"It seems a poor way to inspire any spirit of Christmas merriment," she went on. "Whatever shall I do, since Lord Kirtland seems incapable of civil conversation and forbids me any more congenial company?"

"You might spend some time giving thanks for the fact that you were not seriously injured," said Charles mildly. "After all, Christmas is not just a season for frivolity and fun, but a time to consider our blessings."

As a slow burn rose to her cheeks, Emma suddenly felt a prickling of shame. "Do you really think me so shallow?" she asked in a small voice.

"I am beginning to think that any female is unfathomable for a poor simpleton like me."

"Please don't jest. It's just that. . . it's obvious that Lord Kirtland doesn't like me above half. He looks at me as if. . . as if I was a lump of coal, come blacken the holidays for his family."

Charles laughed. "Then, I shall bring a pair of spectacles for him, along with your things."

Before she could make further protest, he rose and took up his hat and gloves.

"That should ensure that he will not pop you in the stove to warm up the cold winter night."

"Charles!" Her tone became even more plaintive.

"Cheer up. It won't be nearly as bad as you think."

Emma bit back a caustic reply—which proved fortuitous because no sooner had her cousin left the room when another person appeared at the half-open door.

"I understand there has been a dreadful accident," said Anne, venturing a step into the room. "I do hope you are not in too much pain, Lady Emma. You must tell me if there is anything I can do to make you more comfortable."

She quickly bent to fuss with the pillow, gently propping up Emma's freshly bandaged ankle. "I am Noel's—that is, Lord Kirtland's—sister, Mrs. Hartley." A twitch of embarrassment played on her lips. "I am still getting used to the notion of his being a titled gentleman."

Relieved that someone was showing a little sympathy for her plight, Emma managed a wan smile.

Although Mrs. Hartley was dressed in somber black, there was a warmth to her expression, especially in her soft hazel eyes, which were now crinkled in concern.

She was, Emma judged, some years older than herself, though not far past the first bloom of youth. Indeed, with such lustrous raven hair accentuating her delicate features and porcelain complexion, the baron's sister was likely to be thought a very pretty lady by anyone making her acquaintance.

"How kind of you, Mrs. Hartley," she murmured. "I should very much like a cup of tea and some toast. Then, perhaps you might spare some time to sit with me and read—"

"No, Lady Emma, she *cannot* spare the time." Noel paused by the open doorway and added, "I warned you, we are all quite busy enough as it is around here, without having to cater to the whims of one used to being waited on hand and foot."

"Noel!" cried Anne in some surprise. Biting her lip, she then dropped her voice to barely above a whisper. "There is no need to speak so harshly."

Emma noted with dismay that his expression became darker.

"I told you, Anne, I'll not have you forced to play nursemaid to our *exalted guest*."

The emphasis he put on the last two words made it clear he was even less pleased with the situation now than he had been at their first encounter.

"I know you are anxious to choose the material for Toby's room, and there is no reason for you to put it off," continued Noel. "I, too, have some errands that cannot wait, so I have had the gig brought around for a trip into the village."

Emma took pains to hide her embarrassment as he turned her way.

"Our housekeeper will bring you some refreshment when she is done putting fresh linens in one of the spare bedchambers," he said brusquely. "Later, she will fix you a light nuncheon as well. But from this evening on, you will have to take your meals when the rest of us are served, though the fare may be not to your taste."

Goaded on by his rudeness, Emma could not keep a rein on her own tongue. "You need not bite my head off, sir. I wasn't expecting Mrs. Hartley to wait hand and foot on me—I was merely asking if she might be free to help distract me from the pain in my ankle."

Noel's eyes narrowed for a moment, then his glance fell on his sister's workbasket. He took it up and dropped it none too gently within Emma's reach. "You need some distraction? Then pray, why not make yourself useful and mend one of my nephew's stockings."

She stared in confusion at the jumble of darning threads and needles.

"Or perhaps you can't manage so much as a simple stitch." He shrugged. "If not, then you will have to think of something else to amuse yourself." He turned to his sister. "Anne, come along with me. Before we leave, I wish to know your opinion on what color is best for the trim in the dining room."

The young widow shot an apologetic look at Emma before hurrying after her brother.

It was all Emma could do to keep from bursting into tears, more from anger than from any physical injury. Drat the insufferable man! Arrogant, sharp-tongued, unfeeling —it was not *she* who should be put to blush for boorish behavior!

Or should she?

Her throat constricted as she thought back on the events of the morning. Her cousin's warnings had been eminently reasonable, and yet she had paid them no heed. Indeed, she had deliberately flaunted his advice. She swallowed hard. It was exceedingly lucky that a twisted ankle was the worst result of her actions. Her horse might have been seriously injured. Or Charles, who had been obliged to risk his own neck in giving chase to her.

And what about his other chidings?

Emma shifted uncomfortably against the faded chintz cushions of the sofa. It hadn't occurred to her that any of her actions might have caused pain to anyone else. Surely he must know that she would never consciously seek to hurt.

Her chin dropped and she gave a small sniff. That, she suddenly realized, was exactly the point he had been trying to make. As she recalled his little lecture, she saw that he must consider her thoughtless. And no doubt just as arrogant, sharp-tongued and unfeeling as the odious Lord Kirtland.

A tear spilled down her cheek. It was not a pleasant thing to have to contemplate, and it set off a warring of emotions within her. A part of her wished to deny the truth of his words. Her behavior might be less than perfect, she reasoned, but it was wrong of him to bring up such serious matters during a holiday that was meant to be joyous. Nor did her own shortcomings in any way excuse the cold rudeness of her reluctant host.

And yet...

And yet, no amount of reasoning could chase away a most unsettling thought. Perhaps the effusive praise she was receiving from all the gentlemen seeking to curry her favor was indeed turning her into a spoiled brat. It seemed no matter what she chose to do—drive too fast, laugh too loudly, tease too sharply—everyone laughed and encouraged her, calling it a show of high spirits.

In a word, everyone told her she was perfect.

And deep inside, Emma knew all too well that she was not.

She bit her lip in confusion, uncertain on how to sort it all out. Here she was, with peace and quiet in which to think through the conundrum, and yet she wasn't quite sure where to begin.

Between her own depressed state of mind and Lord Kirtland's obvious dislike, how would she ever endure this confinement?

Feeling very small and very alone, she allowed her gaze to wander around the small room, hoping to find any sort of respite from such dismal thoughts. Perhaps there was a book or newspaper that might offer a brief distraction. Though how she would fetch it was another matter.

However, she spotted nothing.

Repressing a sigh, Emma rearranged the wool blanket over her lap and looked around once more. The room was, at least, a pleasant one, with light to stream in through the large mullioned windows, though the second glance did make it clear that the baron had not exaggerated—there was much work to be done to put things in order. The hearth could use another coat of beeswax, the draperies were in need of a good beating to rid them of the dust and the planked floor had a dull scuff of neglect to it.

Perhaps it was no wonder that Lord Kirtland was not in the best of humors, admitted Emma. Heddy looked to be correct for once in guessing that he had not inherited much blunt along with the title and house.

Still, it did not excuse the man's execrable manners—

The thump of a cricket ball bouncing through the doorway drew her from her reveries. It was followed by a small boy, who was so engrossed with retrieving his toy that he nearly collided with the sofa before he noticed there was someone else in the room.

"Oh!" He pushed a shock of tousled hair back from his forehead, and his eyes grew wide. "Are you an angel sent down from Heaven as a Christmas present?" he asked, staring at Emma's face and golden curls.

She smiled faintly in spite of her bleak mood. At least one male of the household did not consider her a termagant. "I'm afraid not. I am simply your neighbor who is here in your drawing room because of a riding mishap."

He looked rather crestfallen. "I thought maybe you had been sent to cheer up Mama," he mumbled. "She cries a lot, when she thinks I don't see her. Uncle Noel says it is because she misses Papa." His lip trembled. "So do I."

"I fear I am hardly cheerful company for your mother or anyone at the moment." Seeing disappointment spread across the boy's features, she quickly added, "But I will do my best to lift her spirits."

That was, of course, assuming she could manage to lift her own. However, her own misfortune suddenly seemed rather insignificant, and she felt a twinge of contrition on recalling her earlier complaints to Mrs. Hartley.

The boy's face brightened a bit, then his gaze fell on her bandaged ankle. "When I must stay abed, Mama always reads to me. Shall I get one of my books and read you my favorite story?" He looked up shyly. "You would only have to help a little with the words."

Emma's lips twitched. "I should like that very much, sir."

He giggled. "I'm not a sir, I'm just Toby!"

"And I am Emma." She smiled. "Fetch your book, Toby, and let us begin."

If truth be told, she usually found her young nieces and nephews rather annoying, but at this point any diversion—even the company of a five-year-old boy—seemed preferable to sitting and stewing alone.

CHAPTER 3

Charles had to clear his throat to gain Emma's attention. "Well, as usual, you have captivated the attention of every male in your vicinity," he remarked dryly as he entered the drawing room and set down several bandboxes on the worn carpet.

Emma gave a low snort, but before she could answer, Toby shot him an aggrieved look.

"You are interrupting the best part of the story!"

"I beg your pardon." Charles took a seat in one of the side chairs and grinned at his cousin. "Do go on."

She finished reading the page aloud, then put the book aside. "We shall start the next chapter in just a bit," she promised, taking in Toby's mutinous expression.

"Oh, very well," allowed the boy.

The grin on Charles's face grew wider. "Perhaps tomorrow I shall bring along some of the picture books from the nursery to keep the two of you occupied." He gestured at the boxes he had brought. "Your maid packed a few essentials while I took the liberty of adding a few books."

He glanced at Toby. "Though the offerings from Minerva Press might not be exactly to your present audience's taste."

"Does the big brown horse I saw this morning belong to you?" interrupted the boy, the awe apparent in his voice.

Charles nodded. "And if you ask your housekeeper for an apple, I shall take you out when I leave and let you feed him the treat."

With a squeal of delight, Toby scurried off as fast as his little legs would carry him.

"I told you it wouldn't be so bad," her cousin said after the boy had quit the room. "You have a gentleman hanging on your every word."

Emma made a face. "You needn't keep reminding me that you think me a vain and selfish creature, Charles."

"I don't—just a bit headstrong at times." He toyed with a fob hanging from his watch chain. "Is there anything else you would like?"

"A ride home," she shot back. "Despite your teasing, there is one gentleman here who, I assure you, is *not* enamored with my presence. I vow, I should not be surprised to find myself relegated to a bed of straw in the stable when night draws nigh. And grudgingly at that."

His brow rose a fraction. "You exaggerate. Kirtland seems quite a solid fellow to me."

She crossed her arms. "I do not." He might be solid, she added to herself, recalling his muscular chest and the corded strength of his arms. But he was not very nice.

"Hmmm," was the only answer her cousin made. After a brief pause, he changed the subject. "Robert is expected to arrive by Friday. He is bringing along a Lord Bryson from Devon. And my friend—you remember Mr. Harkness, from the Fernleigh's ball—arrives this afternoon. "

The conversation continued on for a time on the comings and goings at Telford Manor until Toby, who had been standing at the doorway, could no longer contain his impatience.

"Mrs. Crenshaw has given me an apple," he piped up in a not so subtle reminder.

Charles made a show of consulting his watch. "I do believe my allotted hour is nearly up. Wouldn't want to face the firing squad for disobeying orders, would I, lad?"

He rose. "Perhaps I can contrive to coax permission from his lordship to allow an extra hour tomorrow." He winked. "And maybe I shall smuggle in a sweetmeat or two to supplement the bread-and-water rations."

"If Papa were home, he would not make such a jest of my predicament," she replied.

"The time will pass quicker than you think. After all, it's only for a few more days."

"It's easy enough for you to say," she murmured as he strolled off with Toby.

But indeed, she hardly noticed the passing hours. When Toby returned a short while later, they quickly resumed reading the latest chapter of the swashbuckling adventure.

The boy had climbed up beside her, his small head nestling against her shoulder as he sat listening with rapt attention. Emma was so engrossed in the story that she didn't hear the front door open and shut.

"Oh, Lady Emma, I do apologize if Toby has given you no peace this afternoon." The sight of them together on the old sofa drew a sharp intake of breath from Anne as she peeked into the room. "I am sure you would have much preferred to rest or—"

"Toby has been a delightful companion," assured Emma. "He has helped keep my mind off my injuries."

And the rude manners of the lady's brother, she added to herself.

Anne gave Emma a grateful look. "That is very kind of you to say."

"I read the story to Emma—well, almost all of it," chirped the boy.

Both ladies smiled, then Anne cleared her throat. "Toby, you can't address our guest so informally. You must call her Lady Emma, or milady. It is not proper—"

"Oh, please, it's quite all right," interrupted Emma. "I should very much like for Toby to think of me as a. . . friend."

"Mama," continued Toby. "Emma has been great fun." He cocked his head to one side. "Why did Uncle Noel call her a whiny brat?"

Anne turned a vivid shade of crimson. "Toby!" she gasped in strangled embarrassment. "You must learn *not* to repeat what you overhear adults say, for there is much you, er, misunderstand."

"That's quite all right, Mrs. Hartley. Please don't trouble yourself over it," said Emma softly. "Lord Kirtland has not exactly kept his sentiments a secret. I am sorry that my presence appears to be an onerous burden on your household at this time. If I had any choice in the matter, I assure you I would have taken myself off long ago."

Anne's color deepened. "I apologize for my brother's manners, as well as those of my son. I am ashamed that you have been made to feel so unwelcome." She shook her head. "I don't know what has brought on such unaccountable behavior in my brother—he is usually the soul of politeness."

"You needn't apologize for me, Anne," said Noel, as he came to stand in the doorway. "I am capable of making my own, if necessary."

Anne fixed him with an odd stare for a moment, and seemed on the verge of making some sort of reply. Instead she merely turned and picked Toby up from the sofa. "Come, lambkin, it is way past time for you to have your nap."

"But I haven't shown Emma the spillikins Uncle Noel made for me! Or the painted pony he brought from Spain."

"I should love to see such treasures, but I am a bit fatigued right now. Might it wait until after supper?" said Emma, darting a look at the baron that seemed to challenge him to issue an order to the contrary.

"Oh, very well." The boy's eyes were already half closed, and his head was resting on Anne's shoulder.

As soon as mother and child had quitted the room, Noel took a step closer to Emma. "Do you wish to be taken up to your bedchamber for the evening?" he asked gruffly.

Her chin came up. "Despite your wish for me to be out of your sight, sir, I am not in the least tired and would rather remain where I am. That is, of course, assuming I really do have a choice in the matter."

"Very well. But I warn you that I have a few things in here that I must attend to."

She made a wry face. "Well, I shall try very hard not to get in your way."

To her surprise, a glimmer of a smile twitched on his lips. Instead of taking his leave right away, he shifted his weight from foot to foot and clasped his hands behind his back. "I see I shall have to watch my tongue a good deal more carefully around my nephew from now on. I am sorry that he gave voice to a comment that was not meant to be repeated."

Emma drew in a breath. It was hardly a handsome apology, but as it clearly cost him some effort to make, she supposed she must accept it.

Still, stung by his obvious reluctance, she couldn't resist a less-than-laudable reply of her own. "Ah. You are sorry that Toby repeated it? Or sorry it was said in the first place?"

His jaw tightened. "You may take my words to mean what you wish." With that, he turned on his heel and left.

In a few minutes be was back again, carrying several rags, a tin of beeswax, and a large wooden box. Studiously avoiding any glance in her direction, he stripped off his coat, rolled up his sleeves, and began a vigorous cleaning of the carved pine mantel.

Emma made a show of picking up one of the books that Charles had brought for her. But try as she might, she couldn't keep her gaze from straying to where he was working and watching the way his corded muscles moved beneath the fine linen of his shirt.

To her acute embarrassment, he turned abruptly to reach for another rag and caught her staring.

"Gentlemen are not supposed to engage in such menial tasks," she said sharply to mask her embarrassment.

"As you are well aware, I am not a proper gentleman. At least not the sort of gentleman you are used to," he answered, taking up another dollop of the fragrant wax and rubbing it into the wood.

She couldn't tell whether his expression was a smile or a sneer.

"But in my mind, a true gentleman would not ask another person to do a task which he is not capable of doing himself," added Noel. "I am not ashamed to put an honest effort into making this house a more cheerful place in which to live."

Emma bit her lip as she forced her eyes back to the printed page, realizing that once again she had appeared a pampered and spoiled prig. The thought of it shouldn't bother her in the least—after all, why should it matter what some rough country lord thought of her?

But somehow it did.

She couldn't help but think about why. Another furtive glance at Noel showed him working diligently to polish the wood. He was as different from other gentlemen of her acquaintance as chalk was from cheese. There was a certain strength that radiated from him—not just a physical presence but a sense of character as well. He certainly made no attempt to hide his true self behind a facade of charming manners or amiable wit, like so many bucks of the ton.

And although he presented a hard and impenetrable countenance when he regarded her, the softening of his features when he looked at his sister and nephew revealed that a caring, compassionate nature lay within.

Loath as she was to admit it, she found that much as she wished to dislike him, she found him quite. . .

Admirable. And, if truth be told, quite intriguing.

Her fingers turned the page with a decided snap. Well, she chided herself, there was little need to wonder what he thought of her! He had ignored her presence since making his barbed retort, focusing all his attention on his work. Why, he was even whistling under his breath, as if he was enjoying himself.

She slanted another sidelong glance in his direction and saw that he was finished with the polishing. Putting the rag aside, he drew the wooden box closer and removed a half dozen oranges, a long length of ribbon, scissors, and a glass jar of cloves. He lay all the items on the rug in front of the hearth, then picked up one of the oranges and began to stick the pieces of spice into its skin in a willy-nilly fashion.

The first few went in without mishap, but the next one slipped and pricked the tip of his thumb.

"Damnation," he muttered, giving his finger a shake.

"Perhaps I should remind you about slips of the tongue, sir," she murmured, "lest Toby keep adding to his rapidly expanding vocabulary."

"I beg your pardon," he growled. After another grimace, his mouth quirked upward into a wry grin.

Emma swallowed hard at seeing how the smile brought a certain golden sparkle to his eyes.

"Quite right," he continued. "I doubt Anne would appreciate that sort of progress in his learning." He paused to jab another random spike into the fruit.

"Lord Kirtland, those cloves are supposed to be arranged in a certain order, you know."

His brow furrowed. "They are?"

"Yes. You must make sure that the ribbon can wrap around—oh, here, hand it to me and I'll show you."

He hesitated. "You have made pomander balls before?"

"I have," she said rather wistfully. "My brother Robert and I had great fun making decorations for Christmas when we were children."

"And?"

She thought for a moment. "And then Mama died, and well. . . I suppose the servants did it."

Still, he made no move to give it to her. "You might scrape your delicate skin or break a nail," he warned.

Emma felt a sharp stab of disappointment. She looked down at her book again, hoping that she might hide the glint of a tear that his casual rebuff had brought to her eyes. "If I did, you need not fear that the whiny brat would complain," she replied in a brittle voice. "But of course it is clear that you do not wish my touch to sully anything in your ·precious household."

Taking great care to smooth a crease from one of the pages, she pretended to turn her full attention back to the volume in her lap.

CHAPTER 4

*H*is tongue seemed bent on creating no end of problems today, thought Noel with a rueful grimace. He sat back on his haunches, twining the length of ribbon around his fingers as he cast a sideways look at Emma. The two spots of color on her cheeks and the rigid set of her jaw indicated that despite her show of unconcern, her feelings had been wounded.

His lips compressed. He hadn't meant to be cruel. It was just that her offer had taken him by surprise. So, for that matter, had her behavior with Toby. She had been nice to the lad. And patient, which he well knew was not always easy with an energetic five-year-old.

The trouble was, he wanted to keep thinking of her as naught but a spoiled heiress, for to allow even a hint of regard to develop might be. . .

Dangerous.

He slanted another quick glance at her profile—the rich blue of her eyes, the pert tilt of her nose, the lush fullness of her mouth, and the hint of vulnerability in her expression—then looked quickly away.

Lud, she was quite the most lovely lady he had ever met, and if he were not careful, he would might start behaving like the drab, common moth who finds itself drawn inexorably toward a bright, shimmering flame.

Dangerous indeed.

Uttering a silent oath, he stood up abruptly and held out the orange and the jar of spice.

"I'm sorry," he said gruffly. "That was ill done of me. I would be grateful for your help, if you still wish to offer it."

It was Emma's turn to hesitate. "You needn't ask me just because you feel you should be polite."

Noel allowed a wry smile. "As you may have noticed, I am not overly concerned with the social graces."

She gave a tentative smile in return as she accepted the proffered items. "The thought might have occurred to me."

"Actually, I am simply being pragmatic," he added dryly. Uncorking a can of linseed oil, he began to wipe down the dingy wainscoting around the fireplace. "I could use a hand if I am to finish making things cheery for Anne and Toby by Christmas Eve. It is their first holiday without—" He caught himself. "But that is hardly any of your concern."

"Do I really seem so incapable of caring for anyone except myself?" asked Emma in a tight voice.

"I did not mean—" He felt a flush rise to his cheeks. "That is, I simply did not

mean to burden you with my problems."

Emma already rearranging the nubbed cloves into neat rows. "Was your sister's husband a soldier like you, sir?"

"No, he had a small estate near Lymington. When an epidemic of influenza swept through the area, he and Anne insisted on tending to their servants. "

Though naturally reserved, Noel soon found it was easier to talk to Emma than he had ever imagined. She listened well and asked thoughtful questions. And any doubts that may have lingered as to her character were quickly put to rest by her quick intelligence and lively sense of humor. It was soon clear that she was not the shallow, conceited young lady he had first taken her to be.

And as he managed a bit of probing of his own and learned something of her own background, he found that the outer show of bravado hid a far more sensitive nature. Indeed, the more they talked, the more intriguing she became.

Dangerous. The word once again began echoing a warning inside his head.

Noel barely noticed how much time had passed until Anne and Toby returned, followed by the housekeeper who, along with his sister, was carrying a tray of food.

"Since it would be uncomfortable for you to move to the dining room, Lady Emma, I thought we would join you for an informal supper here," announced Anne, venturing a stern look at Noel as if she expected him to protest.

"An excellent idea," he murmured, standing up and wiping his hands with a clean cloth. "May I fix a plate for you, Lady Emma? You have certainly earned a bit of sustenance with your labors."

Emma laid aside the last of the oranges. "I am almost done with these, so you had best find me another chore so that I may deserve breakfast," she replied in a bantering tone.

Anne ducked her head to hide a small smile, but tactfully refrained from making any comment on the marked change of attitude in both her brother and their guest.

"Emma, Emma! I have brought my spillikins, and my pony for you to see." Toby was quick to climb onto the sofa beside his new friend and dump an armful of wooden toys in her lap.

"Perhaps you would care to dine alone in your room," said Noel quietly. "As Anne said, things tend to be rather more informal here than you are used to."

Emma was already admiring the gaily-painted animals. "I should prefer to stay here," she replied. "That is, if you have no objection to my joining your family meal."

"You are welcome to remain." He handed her a plate, then gathered his nephew in his arms and tossed him up in the air. The little boy shrieked with delight as Noel caught him and turned him upside down.

"Here now bantling, you must leave Lady Emma in peace for a bit."

Toby grabbed at his uncle's knee, and gave a yank to the well-worn top of his boot. Noel pretended to trip, and collapsed to the floor. The two of them wrestled for a few moments before the boy emerged from a tangle of limbs and plopped down on Noel's chest with a thump.

"I give up," cried the baron in mock surrender. "I see I shall have to engage in a series of lessons with Gentleman Jackson himself if I am to have any hope of victory in the future." He sat up slowly and brushed a mass of tangled locks from his brow. No doubt after this display of behavior, Lady Emma would find him to be a very odd sort of gentleman—as well as ill-tempered—compared to the polished, well-mannered bucks of the ton.

And what of it?

Giving an inward shrug, he turned and added another log to the crackling fire, trying to ignore the flicker of desire stirring inside him.

Between Toby's eager chatter and Anne's polite questions to Emma concerning holiday traditions of the area, the meal passed quickly. Noel waved away his sister's offer of help and removed the supper tray himself. When he returned, he brought back her basket of greenery and another box filled with assorted items for fashioning decorations.

Anne hesitated as she picked up a bough of fresh-cut holly. "We could take our work to the kitchen so that we don't disturb you any longer, Lady Emma. You must be rather exhausted."

"Oh, please don't go," replied Emma. "I should hate to miss all the fun."

And good fun it was, she found herself thinking a short time later, when everyone was engaged in making the room look cheery. Noel had begun to hang the clove-scented oranges from the freshly waxed mantel, while Anne was arranging bouquets of fragrant pine boughs in earthenware jugs and along the windowsills.

Meanwhile, Toby was busy cutting out lopsided paper snowflakes with a pair of blunt scissors. The boy's peals of laughter punctuated Noel's gentle teasing of his sister, and a cozy warmth filled the room—not just from the flames dancing high in the newly polished hearth.

How had she thought the baron a cold, unfeeling man? reflected Emma. He was certainly neither. Recalling his playful antics with his nephew and his undisguised concern for his sister, she was moved by the genuine show of his feeling, so unlike the bored ennui affected by many of the gentlemen of the ton.

She paused for a moment in finishing the last pomander ball, and suddenly felt a small knot form inside her chest. There was a palpable spirit of love and kinship surrounding her companions. Lord Kirtland and his family might lack for blunt, but they had something infinitely more valuable, she realized with a start. Something that many people would gladly pay a fortune to possess.

As she watched the flicker of the flames, Emma bit her lip and thought of the endless rounds of balls, routs and house parties she had attended over the last year. And it suddenly struck her that between all the flatteries of her admirers and the swirl of new activities, she had become rather too caught up in the pursuit of superficial pleasures. Her father, her brother and her cousin—she had become so self-absorbed that they had become almost strangers. That the prospect of missing bit of revelry because of a twisted ankle had seemed a dire calamity only showed how shallow her feelings had become.

She felt a sharp pinch of shame on comparing her trifling misfortune to that of Mrs. Hartley.

No wonder Lord Kirtland thought her a spoiled brat.

Emma watched as the baron paused in his labors to

help Toby thread a ribbon through one of his creations. Out of the corner of her eye, she caught sight of Anne staring pensively into the fire, a sad expression stealing to her face as she thought no one was looking.

"Mrs. Hartley," she said after a moment's thought. "Do you and your brother plan to visit London this spring?"

"Why, I—that is, Noel hasn't—" she stammered.

"I daresay you would enjoy it immensely. Though I cannot vouch the same for Lord Kirtland."

Anne looked rather startled.

"No doubt he would be forced to spend much of his time fending off a host of your besotted admirers."

"Oh, w-what an absurd notion," mumbled the young widow in some confusion. Her cheeks, however, took on a pretty pink glow. "I—I am much too old to attract a second glance from a gentleman."

"I would love to show you some of the shops on Bond Street," continued Emma, ignoring the other lady's blushes and stuttering. "I know any number of dressmakers and milliners who would delight in the opportunity to fit someone with such a pretty face and lovely figure."

Anne's blush deepened to a vivid shade of red. "Y-you are simply being kind," she whispered, though it was clear the compliment had affected her deeply. She cleared her throat. "I have read in *La Belle Assemble* that to be fashionable, one must purchase a bonnet at Madame Therese. Is that true?"

"Oh, as to that, I should advise you to visit a little shop off of Bond Street where the prices are not only better, but the styles more flattering and the workmanship superb. "

The two ladies then fell into an animated discussion on fashion, which soon turned into a description of the various balls and assemblies that Emma had attended during the past Season. Anne hung on her every word, and even Toby stopped with his tossing of the spillikins to listen to the descriptions of the colorful gowns, lavish suppers, and the latest music from the Continent.

"London!" cried the little boy when Emma paused for a bit. "Uncle Noel, can we see the horses at Astley's while Mama and Emma dance a waltz? And taste the treats at Gunther's?"

The baron's expression was hidden in shadow. "We shall see, imp."

Before Toby could make any further demands, Noel scooped him up from the floor and tossed him over his shoulder. "Come, give me a hand in fetching more wood for the fire," he said, giving a quick wink at his sister. "I have learned that men are never welcome when the ladies fall to discussing these sorts of topics."

When the two of them returned a short while later, Emma had brought a spark of merriment to Anne's eyes and a smile to her lips with a humorous account of some musicale gone awry when the featured singer had imbibed a glass too many of champagne. The sound of their laughter took several minutes to die down.

"Lady Emma, do tell Noel the story of Mr. Patterson ending up in Lady Chalford's fountain," urged Anne as she stifled another giggle.

"I shall be happy to do so if you are sure he will not be

bored by it—but please, you must simply call me Emma. All my friends do."

The young widow blushed again, this time with pleasure. "I would be happy to do so, if you will do me the honor of calling me Anne."

The intimacies agreed upon, Emma dutifully recounted the requested incident, drawing a chuckle from the baron and a quizzical look from Toby.

"How can a gentleman be in his cups?" demanded the boy. "Even if he were as small as me, he would never fit more than several toes in such tiny things."

"Quite right, lad," replied Noel dryly. "Perhaps in another few years I shall be able to explain to you just how such an odd thing can come to pass. But not now."

"Why not—"

A warning glance from his mother caused the protest to die on his lips. "Oh, very well," finished Toby, trying hard to conceal a yawn.

Not fooled in the least, Anne rose from her chair. "I think that a certain young man is ready for bed," she murmured, watching her son's chin slump to his chest. "If you will excuse us, I shall take him up to his bedchamber."

She flashed a shy smile at Emma. "I am sure that you, too, have had enough excitement for one day. Noel will assist you up to the guest room, and I will be along to help you settle in as soon as I have seen to Toby."

An awkward silence descended over the room once she and the child had left. The baron took up the poker and turned to jab at the dying flames in the hearth while Emma carefully refolded a length of ribbon. A log hissed and crackled as it fell from the andirons, causing her head to jerk up.

"Well, I suppose I had best see you settled for the night, then." He approached the sofa, hands jammed in the pockets of his coat.

Emma felt her cheeks go as red as the glowing coals at the thought of being taken up in his arms again. Embarrassed by how much the idea sent a frisson of heat through her, she shrank back against the cushions.

"M-my ankle is really much better. I am sure I can manage the stairs by myself if you will just steady my arm."

"And risk further injury?" He shook his head, a grim expression coming to his face. "Not a wise strategy, Lady Emma. I, for one, do not wish to have to report to the duke that his daughter's condition was made worse while under my roof by another act of foolishness that I might have prevented."

Like the banked fire, his voice had lost all of its earlier warmth, and the chill of his tone was matched by the rigid line of his jaw.

So, she thought to herself, he must still think of her as a willful, spoiled termagant. No doubt he had been merely feigning the apparent thaw in his feelings in order to please his sister.

Although the notion of it hurt far worse than the throbbing in her ankle, Emma was determined to mask her own true feelings as well as he had done.

"As you are no longer in the military, Lord Kirtland, you need not consider yourself responsible for the actions of those under your command. My father would hardly line you up before a firing squad for dereliction of duty, even if you were at fault," she managed to reply. "So don't worry. You will not s-suffer for my s-sins." To her dismay, the last words were accompanied by a tremble of her lip and the spill of a tear.

"Oh, the deuce take it," she cried in embarrassment, wiping at her cheek with an angry swipe of her sleeve. "Please leave! You have already made it clear I am naught but an onerous burden without another lecture to show how much you loathe my very presence in your house. Anne will help me, or I shall stay here on this sofa for the night. Indeed, I should be happy to crawl to the stable if it meant I could avoid another moment of your grim, disapproving stare!"

Noel's expression, which had indeed been quite grim, changed to one of shocked surprise. "You think I disapprove of you—" he began.

"No—I think you simply despise me." The tears were flowing more freely. "Not that I care at all what you think," she added between watery sniffs.

He took a step closer. "Of course you don't. And why should you, when apparently I have shown myself to be a tongue-tied ass."

There was a shuffling pause while he cleared his throat. "I'm afraid I have little experience with Polite Society, having lived for the most part in the company of plain-speaking soldiers. Please forgive me if my manners appear rough and unpolished in comparison to what you are used to. I—I meant nothing of the sort."

"Oh, you needn't apologize," murmured Emma,

instantly regretting her outburst. No doubt he would now think her more childish than ever. "Rather it is I who should beg pardon for indulging in such a fit of vapors, as well as for becoming a veritable watering pot." A few small drops still clung to her lashes. "I-I am not usually prone to tears."

A ghost of a smile crossed his lips. "I am sure you are not. In fact, you have shown more courage than many of my veteran troops, putting on a brave face with what I know must be a very painful injury."

Ducking her head to hide the blush that his unexpected compliment brought to her cheeks, Emma stammered something unintelligible in return.

"But now I am sure you must be truly exhausted," went on Noel. "Both from discomfort of your ankle and from being pressed into service as a nursemaid and a lowly laborer." His expression twisted into one of wry regret. "I am sorry you did not land in more congenial company, Lady Emma. However, I hope you will at least put up with my grim face long enough that I might see you comfortably settled upstairs."

This time when he bent forward, Emma made no move to sidle away. His arms slipped around her and lifted her from the sofa. The baron was right—his manners and bearing were indeed different from all the other gentlemen of her acquaintance. As her head settled against his shoulder, she realized she couldn't begin to imagine one of the dandies of her set doffing his elegant coat to wrestle with a giggling child. Neither could she picture any of them deigning to mess with cloves and oranges in order to create a Christmas decoration for a mantel he had just cleaned with his own hands.

"I haven't enjoyed anything as much as such labors—as you call them—in a long while," she said softly. There was a shy hesitation. "Or such company."

Noel gave a low chuckle, and she could feel the light tickle of his breath on her neck. "You need not go that far in doing the pretty, Lady Emma. While I, too, find Anne and Toby delightful to be around, I have no illusions about how pleasant my grim visage has been to you."

His tone turned more serious. "As I have said, my skills are sadly lacking when it comes to playing a proper gentleman."

He pulled her closer to his chest on starting up the stairs, and Emma was suddenly aware of the faint tang of orange and clove mixed with the masculine undertones of bay rum and leather. That, along with the heat emanating through the thin linen fabric of his shirt, made her feel a bit light-headed.

" I-I. . ." she stammered in some confusion. "That is, y-you. . ."

The baron appeared to take no notice of her stuttering.

"While you seem to have a knack for putting people at their ease," he went on in a low voice. "For weeks I have been racking my brains for a way to bring a smile and some life to Anne's face, yet you managed it so easily. My thanks—that was truly kind of you."

"Oh, l hardly deserve much credit. No lady on earth can remain blue-deviled when talking of the latest fashions and fancy balls," she jested, though his heartfelt praise had brought a lump to her throat.

"Ah, is that the secret?" His tone was as light as hers. "I shall keep it in mind, though I fear such topics will prove just as difficult as fine manners for a rough country farmer to master."

They had reached the doorway of the guest room, and Noel paused to nudge the door open with his boot. It took only a stride or two to reach the narrow bed. He set her down, then quickly stepped back. "Anne will be in shortly," he said, turning to light the candle on the small pine table. "Is there anything else you have need of?"

Emma hesitated. "Just a list of the tasks I should tackle tomorrow, so that I might continue to earn my keep."

"That, at least, is something I can manage with no difficulty at all. They will be sent up with your water and crust of bread." He allowed a momentary grin. "Good night, then, Lady Emma. You had better sleep well."

"Good night, Lord Kirtland."

Noel pulled the door shut behind him. Lud, had he really made such a fool of himself? His lips compressed as he recalled each and every one of his stilted words. She must truly think him a bumbling nodcock for his brusque manner and lack of polish.

Not that it mattered, he reminded himself. A Diamond of the First Water—and one of the most sought-after heiresses in all of London—was hardly going to take note of an impoverished country baron, no matter how charming or affable he might strive to be.

Especially one with a grim, disapproving visage.

His expression grew even fiercer, though the grimace of disapproval was directed at himself for entertaining, even for an instant, such a silly notion that she might find him. . . agreeable. Just because she had hinted that she had enjoyed the evening, and the company. . .

Don't be an ass, thought Noel.

Of course she had only meant Anne and Toby! And who could blame her, given his offensive behavior? Muttering an oath under his breath, he headed back downstairs. There was still a great deal to accomplish before Christmas Eve, and while he may not have any idea of how to go on in a drawing room, he could at least perform a host of practical skills. But at the moment, the fact that he knew how to loosen the bolt of a stove and concoct a polish for pine did not afford him nearly the same satisfaction as it had yesterday.

CHAPTER 5

"Oh, Toby, do be careful!"

The boy just managed to avoid tangling his feet in the long garland of holly that Emma and Anne had just finished knotting together, but the little hop caused him to tumble headfirst into a basket of pine boughs. The two ladies began to giggle as he righted himself, a profusion of green needles clinging to his sable curls.

"Why, he looks the very picture of a Christmas imp," remarked Emma as her laughter subsided.

"And is quite likely to wreak some mischief before the day is done," said Anne with a smile. "Come, Toby. If you wish to be of help, you may hold the end of this holly rope while I arrange it over the dining room mantel."

She turned to Emma and added in a lower voice, "I am sure that you would welcome a bit of peace and quiet, along with a respite from such mundane labors."

Emma waved off her new friend's tentative words. "Nonsense! If you will pass me the ribbon box and the pine boughs, I shall start on the garlands for over the windows while you are busy in the other room."

"But the sap is quite sticky. And the needles can be terribly prickly."

"Yes, and the berries from the holly can make a gooey mess." Emma wiped a smudge of red from her nose and grinned. "No doubt I already look as gloriously disheveled as Toby, so I have no intention of missing out on the fun in order to avoid wreaking further havoc on my appearance."

Anne looked a trifle unconvinced, but as Toby was already tugging on the twined leaves and threatening to undo all their hard work, she let out a small sigh. "Very well. However, I shall not be long."

Once alone, Emma brushed an errant curl from her cheek and took a moment to survey the small parlor. Its transformation was nearly complete—the woodwork glowed with its fresh coat of fragrant wax, the mantel was festooned with greenery, the brass fender gleamed like a newly minted coin in the reflection of the roaring fire, and the spicy scent of oranges and cloves perfumed the air. Even the draperies had lost their coating of dust, though the baron must have risen at dawn to have managed the task.

All that was left to do was arrange the swags of pine boughs above the painted casements.

Her brow slowly furrowed as she watched the cheery flames dance up from the burning logs in the hearth. Strangely enough, though the room was hardly larger than the sewing room at Telford Manor, it seemed so much cheerier than the vast formal drawing room where she and her family were accustomed to celebrating Christmas.

Emma looked around once more, trying to puzzle out why. The decorations at the Manor were exquisitely tasteful—hothouse flowers spilled from cut-crystal vases, the greens were always wrapped with expensive ribbon and arranged in perfect symmetry around the windows, while all manner of exotic fruits filled the silver epergnes.

But somehow, in comparison with the lopsided paper stars cut by Toby, the simple stoneware crocks of pine and holly, and the slightly crooked rows of cloves stuck into the oranges, they seemed rather. . . spiritless. It was, she admitted, as if her home, though perfect in outward appearance, had grown hard and cold with the lack of laughter and sharing.

Lud, now she thought about it, when was the last time she and her father and brother had spent more than a fleeting moment with one another's company over the past few months? The answer caused her frown to deepen. She had become so engrossed in her own concerns that she had not given a thought to. . . well, to a great many things, it seemed.

"Sorry," said Noel gruffly, as Emma flinched at the sound of the logs dropping into the wooden box by the hearth. "But I wished to bring in another load in case it begins to snow." He brushed some bits of bark from his sleeve. "I trust your ankle is not worse this morning?"

With a start, Emma realized she had forgotten all about her injury. "On the contrary, sir, I have not felt the slightest bit of discomfort."

The comers of his mouth gave a slight twitch. "Perhaps if you give such a convincing reply to Dr. Dumberton, you might be able to persuade him to release you from confinement sooner than expected."

Biting her lip, she forced herself to ignore the pinch of disappointment caused by his apparent wish to be rid of her. "Speaking of confinement," she replied, "I was wondering whether you might allow more than one visit by my cousin today, as well as permission for him to bring a friend with him this afternoon."

All trace of humor disappeared from the baron's face, and his shoulders stiffened.

"Ah, I suppose it is not to be wondered at, that you have tired of the company of—"

"No!" she protested. "That is not what I meant at all. What I was thinking was, Charles has invited a friend down from Sussex. A widower, actually, with a daughter only a year or two younger than Toby. Mr. Harkness is a very nice gentleman, and it occurred to me that the two of them might provide pleasant company for Anne."

She hesitated for a moment. "It would do her good to meet other people and see a spark of admiration in the eye of a gentleman other than her brother."

Not, she added to herself, that she would *ever* see the light of such sentiment from Lord Kirtland.

Noel's hand tightened on the log he was straightening. "I-I beg your pardon, Lady Emma," he said after a moment or two. "It is a most thoughtful idea. If your cousin is agreeable to the plan, he and his friend are welcome to come by whenever they wish."

Moving with great deliberateness, he finished arranging the rest of the wood in a neat order, then rose and left the room without a further word.

The pine needles suddenly felt like hedgehogs beneath her fingers. Was the baron always so prickly, or was it only her presence that brought out such behavior? Despite the occasional lowering of his spines, he seemed determined to treat her as naught but an unwelcome intruder. Blinking back the sting of tears, she began to fashion a festive bow for one of the garlands, even though her spirits had been sadly flattened.

THE DEVIL TAKE IT! Noel threw down the chisel and rubbed at his scraped fingers. It seemed he was all thumbs at everything he attempted this morning! Not only was the groove for the larder hinge now looking a bit crooked, but once again he had shown himself incapable of behaving with even a hint of gentlemanly civility.

Emma must think him an idiot.

Shoving aside the rest of his tools, he rose and stalked toward the kitchen door. Perhaps a spell outside chopping wood might help relieve some of his pent-up frustration—as well as cool the heat that was coursing through his veins every time he thought of the lovely young lady temporarily marooned under his roof.

It was one thing to ignore her when she seemed no more than a willful brat, but now that she had shown herself to be thoughtful and perceptive and kind to boot...

He swore again under his breath, reminding himself that to let his mind stray in such a direction was unwise.

Thwack. The ax split the log neatly in two. No, it would be best to keep both his thoughts and his person well away from the young lady. Surely it should not be so difficult to avoid her—or at least feign indifference to her presence. After all, she would be gone in another day or two.

But he feared she would haunt his dreams for a good deal longer than that.

". . . and don't forget, there are a number of things that I want you to bring along when you return with Edgar."

Charles regarded his cousin with bemused amazement. It was not merely the sight of the pine needles sticking to her fingers or the faint smudge of red across her cheek or the scraps of cut ribbon and paper clinging to her elegant gown that had rendered him momentarily speechless. Rather it was the striking change in her demeanor since the accident.

"Have Larkins fetch down the box of lead soldiers from the attic, for I know Toby will be in alt at having his very own army to maneuver," continued Emma. "And gather up the last few issues of *La Belle Assemblee*, for Anne will greatly enjoy seeing the very latest fashions from Town."

She tapped at her chin. "Oh—and ask Mrs. Hawkins for a tin of her special wood polish, along with the recipe, for Lord Kirtland. . . " Her voice faltered a little. "That is, Lord Kirtland no doubt has his own preferences, but perhaps he might find it useful."

Was this the same headstrong young lady who had sat there only twenty-four hours ago beseeching him not to leave her in such a dreadful place?

Repressing a grin, Charles couldn't help but wonder whether she had suffered a severe knock on the head as well as a nasty twist of her ankle. If so, he found himself hoping the effects would be a good deal more lasting than the damage to her leg. But he wisely forbore voicing such thoughts aloud.

Giving a slight cough, he merely nodded. "Is that all?"

"Actually it's not." She smiled. "Please have Cook make up a basket of her cakes and perhaps a pigeon pie and a crock of her stewed mushrooms. And why not include a bottle or two of Papa's favorite claret! We are busy enough here without Anne or the housekeeper having to make supper."

At this remark, Charles couldn't resist an arch of his brow as he regarded her slightly disheveled state. "Hmm, yes. Busy, indeed."

Emma gave a rueful grimace as she brushed a strand of hair off her forehead, then looked down at her grubby hands and the scraps clinging to the folds of her gown.

"I suppose I hardly look like the proper lady, but there is much to do to get this house ready for Christmas, and it was clear they could use an extra hand."

"So, it does not appear as if you are suffering from the ennui or deprivation that you feared," he murmured.

It was true. She had been so involved in helping the baron's family that her thoughts had been far too occupied to dwell on her own imagined travails. Unsure of how to respond, Emma turned to avoid his inquiring gaze.

"In fact, you and Edgar will be able to help Lord Kirtland move the cupboard in the kitchen. I overheard Anne say that she wished for it to be shifted to the other side of the room, but it requires more than one man." Her brow furrowed in thought. "And no doubt there are a number of other heavy tasks that might be done while you two are here."

"I shall warn my friend that we are expected to provide more than just our scintillating presence." Charles took up his hat and gloves. "Well, I had best take my leave now." There was a slight pause as he tugged the soft York tan leather over his fingers. "How fortuitous for all involved that you landed here."

Emma felt a small pinch in her chest. Though her cousin might not have noticed, it was quite evident to her that not everyone at Hawthorne House would agree with that sentiment.

NOEL SAT off to one side and stared into the crackling fire. A burble of laughter came from the ladies as Charles finished another humorous anecdote concerning the surreptitious addition of a bottle of brandy to the ratafia punch at Lady Atwater's ball. He forced a smile as well, though he had not really been listening.

It was proving nigh on impossible to ignore Lady Emma. Throughout the afternoon, she had required his presence as one task after another had been drawn up to prepare for the evening visitors. Her animated banter and gay laughter had kept everyone in high spirits—including himself.

But perhaps tonight, if he kept his gaze averted from her mesmerizing beauty, he would not feel so much like a lowly moth being drawn toward a flame.

It was, of course, too late to keep his heart from being singed.

How ironic, he thought with an inward grimace. The seasoned officer, who had come through countless battles unscathed by bullet or saber, had been brought to his knees by Cupid's arrow. He was, however, determined to nurse his wound without becoming the object of amusement or pity.

No one would have reason to guess the true state of his feelings.

Another laugh from Anne caused his expression to soften for an instant. The undisguised change in her behavior was cause for silent celebration, no matter his own depressed spirits. Noel slanted a quick glance at her animated face and shy smile. She had clearly made the first tentative steps toward emerging from her shell, encouraged by the kind attentions of Emma and the two affable gentlemen.

Why, Anne had even managed a coherent conversation with Mr. Harkness while the two of them had been engaged in hanging one of the pine swags. Although the talk had been mainly about the sorts of mischief young children were apt to create, it was a start.

He took a sip of his wine. Perhaps Toby's innocent

observation had been correct—perhaps Lady Emma was indeed a Yuletide angel sent down from the heavens in answer to his prayers.

No matter that she would bedevil his peace of mind far longer than the holiday season.

"I hope that we might be permitted to call on the morrow and offer further assistance," said Mr. Harkness, rising reluctantly as the clock on the mantel chimed the lateness of the hour. "I heard mention of chairs needing to be moved down from the attic, and there is still the Yule log to be cut."

"And you may bring more jam tarts!" cried Toby. He shot a pleading look at his mother. "Oh, do say yes, Mama!"

Anne ruffled her son's hair. "The duke's cook has been far too generous as it is." She picked at a fold in her skirts. "And I am sure the gentlemen have far more interesting things to do than to—"

"Why, not at all," interrupted Mr. Harkness quickly. "In fact, the Manor is rather quiet as the duke and Robert have been delayed in London. We would much prefer the company of two charming ladies to another endless round of billiards, wouldn't we, Charles?"

"Of course," agreed Emma's cousin.

"Well, in that case. . ." Anne turned to Noel.

"I should be glad of any help you care to offer," he replied politely. Then he, too, gave a glance at the clock and rose abruptly. "Now, if you will excuse me, there are some matters I must attend to before it grows much later."

·   ·   ·

"Dear me," murmured Mr. Harkness after the door had fallen closed. "Did I say something amiss?"

"Oh, it's not you, Edgar," said Emma with a forced smile. "It's me. I'm afraid Lord Kirtland has formed quite a low opinion of me—"

Charles coughed. "Well, he did have ample reason."

"—and now he finds it difficult to be in the same room with me," she finished softly.

"Surely you exaggerate," exclaimed Mr. Harkness with an odd quirk of his lips. "From what I observed this afternoon, my impression is that Lord Kirtland does not find your company unwelcome."

"I assure you I do *not* exaggerate." She wiggled the toes of her bandaged ankle. "You are quite mistaken. He trying very hard to be polite. But the truth is, he can't wait for me to be out from under his roof."

Her cousin tactfully refrained from further comment.

Anne, too, remained silent, though a pensive expression drew her brows together for an instant as she stared first at the closed door, then at Emma.

"If you don't mind, I should like to be taken up to my room," said Emma after an awkward pause. She lowered her head so that none of the others could see her expression. "I am suddenly feeling very fatigued."

Charles was quick to comply with her request and carried her upstairs without indulging in any more of his usual teasing. He returned in time to catch Anne's puzzled sigh as she rose to accompany the two gentlemen to the door.

"I can't for the life of me figure out what has Noel

acting so strangely," she murmured. "He is not usually given to such unaccountable shifts of mood."

"Emma, too, is behaving quite oddly," remarked Charles.

Mr. Harkness gave a short cough. "I am, of course, a stranger to them both, but it seemed to me that, well, maybe. . . if you take my meaning."

Charles stroked at his chin. "By Jove, do you think it possible?"

"Are you saying. . ." Anne's eyes lit up. "Oh, wouldn't that be wonderful!"

"Wonderful, indeed," repeated Charles, a sly grin stealing to his lips. "Though it appears that the two parties involved are being deucedly stubborn about the whole matter." He pursed his lips. "Hmmm. We'll have to see what can be done to help things along."

THE NEXT FEW days were filled with a whirlwind of activity that somehow required Noel to spend a good deal of time in consultation with his injured guest. The others seemed to need both of their opinions in making the final decisions for a number of minor details. The result, however, was that the inhabited wing of Hawthorne House was looking more like a true home with every passing moment. Every room had been scrubbed and polished, right down to the last nail head, and a profusion of Christmas greenery in gaily beribboned crocks enlivened the freshly dusted chintzes. Even the hallway leading to the kitchen bore a fresh coat of paint, as volunteered by the visitors from Telford Manor.

The project had engendered quite a few giggles from the ladies, as it seemed that more of the pigment had ended up on the two gentlemen and their small helper than on the plaster itself. But all agreed that the end result was a vast improvement over the former dingy shade of soot gray.

Charles and Edgar—everyone had asked Mr. Harkness to drop the more formal use of his last name—insisted on bringing hampers of food prepared by the duke's cook for when the work was done, so suppers turned into a shared affair as well. Fortified with an ample supply of excellent champagne from the cellars of His Grace, the meals passed in an effervescence of good spirits. If Noel and Emma were a trifle more sober than the others, it was not remarked upon—at least not aloud.

That evening, Toby had been put to bed, and the adults had moved to the parlor for a celebration of sorts. The cast-iron stove had finally yielded to the ministrations of three muscular gentlemen and now burned without filling the kitchen with a cloud of smoke.

Noel, as had become his habit, took a seat slightly apart from the others and allowed the others to carry most of the conversation, though Charles and his friend took great pains to draw him out.

"Was that Dr. Dumberton's gig that I spied leaving as we were returning with the last load of cut holly?" asked Charles, after recounting the latest bits of news from the London newspapers. His eyes had strayed to Emma's ankle, which was propped up on a hassock. Showing from beneath the folds of fine merino was evidence of a new—and much less bulky—bandage.

"Yes." She took pains to study the myriad tiny bubbles fizzing to the surface of her drink. "In fact, he says that I am recovered enough to return home on the morrow."

"Well, now, that certainly calls for a toast, doesn't it?" he replied with great heartiness.

She raised her glass, a crooked smile upon her lips. "Yes. Of course."

The others joined in with murmured congratulations.

Noel was the last to speak. "What good news, indeed," was his enigmatic comment. He swallowed the contents of his glass in one gulp, then reached over for the bottle and refilled it to the brim.

His sister fixed him with an odd look before turning away. A small sigh slipped from her lips. "It will seem very. . . quiet without you here." A flicker of hesitation stirred beneath her lashes. "All of you," she said added softly.

"As to that. . ." Edgar cleared his throat. "Er, seeing as, er, you might have a bit of free time, I thought you—and Toby—might like to go for a drive tomorrow afternoon. My daughter has finished the visit with her grandparents, and is coming to join me in the morning. I. . . well, I should like very much for you to meet her. Assuming, of course, that you would care to."

Anne's cheeks took on a very becoming shade of rose. "Oh, I would. Very much so." She darted another quick glance at her brother. "That is, if you are sure there is nothing pressing?"

"Not at all." Noel smiled. Then, as on the previous evenings, he made to rise and quit the room before the others, leaving one of the other gentlemen to assist Emma upstairs.

But this time, Charles forestalled his exit by getting to his feet first. "Edgar, we really must be off now," he announced, making a show of consulting his pocket watch. "Uncle Ivor is due to arrive sometime later tonight, and it would be quite rude if we were not there to greet him."

His friend shot up too. "I shall pack up the hampers and help you take them out to the carriage. No doubt Cook will have need of all her platters now that the holidays are beginning in earnest."

Anne quickly followed their lead. "It has been a long day, and I am sure all of us are quite ready to retire." Without further ado, the three hastened toward the door.

THE DEVIL TAKE IT! Noel shifted uncomfortably in his chair, his gaze riveted on the dancing flames. Taken aback at being left alone with Emma, he was still trying to compose his thoughts when she stirred from her seat and lowered her ankle from its resting place.

"It has been a long day," she murmured, echoing Anne's words. "I believe I shall follow her suggestion and bid you good night, sir."

"Lady Emma, just what do you think you are doing?"

She hesitated. "Why, I am going upstairs. The doctor said—"

Before she could finish, Noel rose from his seat and lifted her up in his arms.

"T-that is quite unnecessary, sir," she stammered. "I am permitted to move about on my own, if I exercise a modicum of caution."

"Since caution does not seem to be your strong suit, I prefer to ensure there are no further accidents."

There was no sting to the words, as they had been uttered with an unexpected gentleness.

Emma glanced up in some surprise, then she quickly looked away. "What you mean is, it would be your worst nightmare were a slip to delay my departure." Though she tried to keep her tone light, there was a small catch in her voice.

Ha! The only nightmare that promised to plague his dreams was the thought of never seeing her angelic face again!

Noel knew he would be treading on dangerous ground if he ventured a reply, but suddenly his steps stilled on the stairs.

Perhaps it was because he had imbibed more of the champagne than usual that prompted him to speak. "You think I shall be glad that you are gone?"

"O-Of course," she replied in a small voice. "You said yourself that my leaving on the morrow was good news indeed."

"We seem to be in the habit of misunderstanding each other's words, Lady Emma," he murmured, his face only inches from hers. "What I meant was, it must be good news indeed for *you*. I remember quite clearly how, on the morning of the accident, you lamented being forced to miss all the fun."

He drew in a ragged breath. "Well, rather than being stuck in this isolated house any longer, you will soon be back in the whirl of fashionable balls and dinner parties, surrounded by your ardent admirers—who are all, no doubt, a good deal more charming and amusing than a grim-faced ex-soldier."

"Perhaps I have come to realize that it is much more important to be surrounded by people who truly care for each other than to be flattered with flummeries by a crowd of fawning strangers," replied Emma.

Her cheek came to rest against his shoulder, then she spoke again, in hardly more than a whisper. "Just as I have come to recognize that you possess a good deal more than charm and bon mots, Lord Kirtland. You are all the things a true gentleman should be. Y-You are caring, compassionate, forthright, and unselfish. Due to your efforts, Hawthorne House has become a true home, and I shall miss. . . everyone here."

She expelled a soft sigh. "I know you still think of me as a nuisance, if not a spoiled brat, but I am hoping that, in the spirit of Christmas, we might part as. . . friends."

"It has been quite some time since I have thought of you as a brat," he replied slowly, tightening his arms ever so slightly and drawing her closer to his chest.

The subtle fragrance of fresh lavender, mingled with a hint of orange, was even more intoxicating than the sparkling wine. And so was the heady notion that her opinion of him was not entirely negative.

For an instant, he feared his own feet might slip out from under him. But then again, be thought with a rueful grimace, he had already fallen hard for the young lady. However, cold reason quickly reasserted itself, and he reminded himself that only a lovesick fool would think her words were anything more than a casual compliment.

To a friend.

Forcing his features to remain impassive, he went on in a measured voice. "Indeed, you have been all that is kind and thoughtful in regard to Anne, not to speak of all your tireless labors. I am most grateful." Realizing he was standing still as a statue, Noel forced himself to continue up the stairs. "It would be most churlish of me to refuse your generous offer, so by all means, let us take our leave on a cordial note."

"Cordial. Yes. I see." She blinked, the fringe of her lashes hiding her eyes. "No doubt you will be engaged in some task when Charles comes around with the carriage tomorrow, so perhaps we should say our good-byes now."

Noel wished he could see her expression, but her gaze had dropped to the treads.

"Thank you for your hospitality, Lord Kirtland," went on Emma as he reached the landing. "You have been most patient in hosting an unexpected visitor."

They approached the door of her bedchamber. After an awkward pause, Noel set her on her feet and stepped back.

"Rather it is I who owe you thanks, for you have brought a good deal of cheer to this place with your presence, Lady Emma," he replied in a voice that he forced to remain neutral. Resisting the urge to gather her once again in his arms and kiss her witless, he took her hand and grazed his lips lightly over her fingers. "May you have a very Merry Christmas."

"And you, sir." Emma reached for the latch, but the door suddenly yanked open and a small, drowsy face peeked out from behind the polished pine.

"Oh, you've come at last!"

"Toby!" cried both of them in unison.

"Imp, what sort of mischief is this?" added Noel.

"It is way past your bedtime and your mother—" began Emma.

"But she said I might wait up for my kiss!" The boy pointed at a sprig of green that hung by a slender ribbon from the top of the door molding. "Mama and Mr. Harkness gathered a great bunch of those funny-looking toes on their walk this afternoon. They said that it makes people who stand under it kiss each other."

He giggled. "Mama said I might have a piece of my own to hang where I wanted, and Lord Lawrance helped me with the hammer and nail. I put it over Emma's door so that she would have to give me a special good-night kiss before she enters."

"And you shall have it." She bent down and hugged him close, then planted a kiss on each cheek.

"Sweet dreams, lambkin."

Until that moment, Noel would never have believed it possible for a seasoned officer to be jealous of a five-year-old.

"Now, off to bed with you, young man, lest you fall asleep on your feet," ordered Emma, giving Toby a last squeeze before directing him toward his room. After watching the little boy disappear around the corner, she started to rise, but her ankle buckled slightly, causing her to take a sharp intake of breath.

Noel was at her side in an instant, his arms slipping around her waist to steady her progress as he lifted her up.

"Have you reinjured yourself?" he asked in concern.

Emma forced a wan smile. "No, no. It was just a momentary twinge."

"Are you sure?" As Noel looked searchingly at her face, he couldn't help but note an elongated shadow shading her cheek. Somehow the two of them had come to be standing directly under the suspended mistletoe, and the silhouette of its delicate leaves and berries flickered across her alabaster skin.

He leaned closer. "P-perhaps you should allow me to carry you the rest of the way."

"Oh, that is not really necessary, sir. As I have said, I have been burden enough on you."

Her mouth, just inches from his, gave an odd little quirk.

For once in his life he decided to throw all caution to the wind. If a five-year-old could so easily request a kiss from the lady of his affections, then surely an experienced officer should be able to muster the courage to do the same.

After all, if he had not enough spirit to take the chance of declaring himself, then he deserved to have her walk out of his life without a backward glance.

His lips came down upon hers with a gossamer touch.

For an instant he feared she was about to use her good foot to boot him head over heels back down the stairs. But then, with a muffled sigh, she tilted her head back and allowed her mouth to soften under his.

The kiss ended all too quickly for his liking, as Emma drew back in some confusion.

"B-but, sir, you don't even like me! You think me. . . a. . . a. . ."

"A sweet angel," he finished. "One who has touched all of us with your warmhearted spirit. But most of all me."

Her lashes lowered. "Y-You are just being gentlemanly."

"If I were a true gentleman, my dear Emma," murmured Noel, "I should not be doing this." He kissed her lightly, first one cheek, then the other, then full on the mouth, where his lips lingered for a lengthy interval.

"But I can no longer keep my true feelings hidden away and risk having you walk—or hobble—out of my life. Do you think you might come to feel some regard for a grim-faced country farmer, with no Town polish?"

Emma placed her hands on his shoulders and drew him into another embrace.

It was some minutes later before he recovered his equilibrium.

"You realize, my love, that I have only a modest inheritance and this small manor to offer you?" he added.

"I am well aware of what you have to offer, Lord Kirtland. And it is infinitely more precious than any of the things of which you speak."

"Still, I would be remiss if I didn't remind you that it will be rather crowded here, compared to what you are used to," he continued. "Anne and Toby do have a home here as well."

A twinkle came to her eye. "Their company will always be most welcome, but judging from how Edgar behaved while helping your sister hang the mistletoe in the front hall, I have a feeling they may be well on the way to having a home of their own again."

Noel grinned. "Why, that would be splendid news indeed. He seems a very fine fellow."

"Very fine," agreed Emma. "There is, of course, no need to mention to either of them that they neglected to shut the door while engaged in their efforts." She brushed back a shock of dark hair from his forehead. "I trust you aren't going to suggest any other drawbacks, else I might start to think you are trying to drive me away."

He hoped the ardor of the embrace that followed put to rest such a ridiculous notion.

"Good Lord, no," he said softly as his lips reluctantly raised from hers. "I just want you to be sure you don't mind that I can't offer you fancy gowns or glittering jewels for Christmas. Only my love."

"That, my dearest Noel, is the most wondrous gift I have ever received."

"Well? What's happening?"

Edgar edged a little farther around the corner of the house and craned his neck so that he might see up to the dimly lit window. "Nothing. . . no, wait! He is. . . bending toward her."

"Thank goodness!" sighed Anne, her breath turning into puffs of white in the chill night air. "I thought he would never admit, even to himself, that his heart was engaged."

"Now what?" asked Charles with some urgency.

"I can't quite make out. . . Or is she?. . . Yes!" exclaimed Edgar. "She is kissing him back!"

"That's the spirit, Emma," murmured Charles. "Always knew that despite your penchant for taking occasional tumbles, your innate good sense would prevail."

He pulled a fresh bottle of champagne from inside his coat and popped the cork. "Now we truly have something to celebrate." After a prolonged swallow, he passed it to Edgar.

"To friends and family, old and new!" said Edgar, giving a wink in Anne's direction as he took a generous nip and handed the spirits back to Charles.

She repressed a laugh on watching the two of them become increasingly unsteady on their feet.

"Well, well. It appears that it's going to be a very merry Christmas indeed!"

ALSO BY ANDREA PICKENS

TRADITIONAL REGENCIES

INTREPID HEROINES

The Banished Bride

The Storybook Hero

Second Chances

A Stroke of Luck

A Lady of Letters

The Defiant Governess

The Major's Mistake

Code of Honor

The Hired Hero

Pistols At Dawn

DANGEROUS LIASIONS

A Diamond in the Rough

Sweeter than Sin

Devil May Care

REGENCY SPY/ADVENTURE/ROMANCES

MRS. MERLIN'S ACADEMY FOR EXTRAORDINARY YOUNG LADIES
The Spy Wore Silk

Seduced by a Spy

The Scarlet Spy

To Love a Spy

OTHER

Omnibus

Christmas by Candlelight

ABOUT THE AUTHOR

I started creating books at the age of five, or so my mother tells me. And she has the proof—a neatly penciled story, the pages lavishly illustrated with full color crayon drawings of horses and bound with staples—to back up her claim. I have since moved on from Westerns to writing about Regency England (clearly I have a thing for Men In Boots!) a time and place that has captured my imagination ever since I opened the covers of Jane Austen's "Pride and Prejudice."

I have a BA and an MFA in Graphic Design from Yale University, where I studied book design (As you see, I've always had a left brain-right brain love affair with art and the printed word.) These days, when I'm not tethered to my keyboard I enjoy traveling to interesting destinations around the world—however, my favorite spot is London, where the esoteric museums, funky antique markets and used book stores offer a wealth of inspiration for my stories.